Emmitt at Love

Gene Lee

Emmitt at Love

Copyright © 2023 by Gene Lee

This is a work of fiction. Any resemblance to actual persons, living or dead, is purely coincidental.

ISBN: 9798987129685

Library of Congress Control Number: 2023935876

Cover Design by All Things that Matter Press

Cover photo: ATTMPress & AI

Author photo is courtesy of Robert Wilcoxson

Published in 2023 by All Things that Matter Press

For Donna and Allison, the two best parts of my world

Acknowledgments

All thanks to Phil and Deb Harris for publishing my work! And to Suzanne Fox who has been the best editor a writer could have and who showed me the proper structure of this novel.

Special thanks to Bob Wilcoxson who turned me on to the joys of fishing the waters of the New England coastline and to Jack Latrobe who willingly and happily joined Bob and me on our adventures there.

Prologue

In the fall of 2000 Emmitt Raines went to Squanocket—just as he had been doing for the last twenty-odd years. He saw no reason not to. New England, the island off the Cape, fishing the month long Derby Days—it's what he did that time of the year. Besides, by going north for the Derby he might begin the healing process. That's what he'd read, more than once, in any one of the various health magazines available to pass the time as he waited for Dana at the doctor's office. The bottom line, according to these magazines, one had to grieve and then let it go before one could begin to heal.

Only, it had never been *his* healing Emmitt was concerned with. Dana, gone close to six months and all the nice words said, the pretty flowers long wilted and thrown away, one afternoon in early September, he decided that maybe he *should* concern himself with some personal healing. Or perhaps he was just worn out from the unusually hot summer Ft. Lauderdale suffered with that year. In the past he had been able to write his way out of things that bothered him. But not now. The words wouldn't come—and besides, he didn't want them to. So it was clear to him that one way or the other, something had to change.

With that thought in mind Emmitt picked up the phone, called Delta, and booked a round-trip flight to Boston. From Logan he'd take the bus to the Cape and catch the afternoon ferry over to Squanocket. Everything settled, and seeing that it was four o'clock, he made himself a drink. It was earlier in the afternoon than he usually started, but what was the old saying? And he did have something to celebrate. It was good enough for him.

As he was making his drink he caught his reflection in the mirror above the wet bar on the porch where he kept the hard liquor. All in all, for a fifty one year old man—a fifty one year old widower—he didn't think he looked too bad. A little more gray showed in his black hair. Hair, now that Dana wasn't around to bug him about it, he kept cut very close, almost in a military style. The dark eyes staring back at him from the mirror seemed clear and bright enough. Of medium height, his weight the same as when he graduated high school, he definitely looked fit. Swimming every day at the beach helped. A morning swim was a habit he and Dana had acquired when they bought the two story house in the Isles section of town. With the house only a ten minute drive from the beach, the two of them had felt it seemed a shame not to take advantage of it.

Not at first—he hadn't done much of anything in the days immediately following Dana's passing—but after a couple of weeks Emmitt had resumed their morning habit. The cool salt water made him forget for a little while. Forced him to focus on the immediate as well as easing his hangover from the day and night before.

Not exactly a conscious decision at the time, he had embarked on a month-long bender after the funeral. A bender that finally ended when the phone rang one afternoon. For once Emmitt actually answered it. It was his friend and agent, Howard Kamen, shouting over the line. "What the fuck are you doing, man?"

Emmitt respected Howard more than any other man he knew—except Huff Larsen, and he was dead. The tone in his friend's voice that afternoon was like one of those Zen koans. But instead of enlightenment, Howard's angry question snapped Emmitt back into sobriety. He wondered for a few days afterwards how Howard, fifteen hundred miles away at his office in New York, had known what he'd been up to. But he was hesitant to ask, superstitious in a way, of breaking whatever spell Howard had cast on him. And the spell had worked, leaving Emmitt somewhat sober again, as well as healthy and alive. Being alive, it was time—past time—he started acting like it.

Three weeks later, with a cold wind blowing in from the harbor, he walked off the boat in Ferry Town, the largest of the three communities on Squanocket. Rory had the room above the bike shop ready for him, and it felt good to get out of the cold wind as he followed the younger man up the stairs to the converted attic loft. The room was a comfortable and functioning space, complete with kitchenette and small bath, plus a great view of Ferry Town harbor. A wooden ship's berth was built into one wall with a firm mattress atop it. The berth was roomy for one person and if necessary, quite capable of accommodating two. The sturdy, rectangular oak table in the center of the room held a lamp. A small bookcase stuffed with paperbacks and charts of the surrounding waters sat on the other end.

Emmitt vividly remembered the first time he and his wife sat down to dinner in the little loft apartment. After ladling heaping spoonfuls of beef stew into the pewter plates the landlord provided, Dana lit two candles and set them in the center of the table. The light from the tapers flickered in the small room. Dana said it first, and Emmitt agreed, that it was like they were on a boat at anchor, listening in their tiny cabin to the sound of the tide flowing into the harbor coming through the open porthole. When the meal was finished they sat together in silence, drinking wine and staring out the window where the winking of scattered mast head lights was the only evidence anything existed in the darkness stretching away from the room.

It had been a time when Emmitt was secure in the world—a time when he'd been young and in love, and loved in return.

"Everything look okay, Mr. Emmitt?"

"Just fine, Rory. Thanks." He'd forgotten Rory was still in the room. "You keep it like your dad did. Clean and ship shape. Huff would be proud."

"Yeah? I like to think so. Didn't have to do much, though, to get her ready. No one's stayed here since Dad's accident. You're the first."

"I'll say it again, then. Good job."

Emmitt had known Rory since he was a kid. A twelve year old with bright red hair who tagged along with his dad and Emmitt when they fished the Cut and the other waters on the island. Emmitt had often thought if he'd had a son he'd want him to be like Rory. And a girl? That was easy enough—like Dana, of course. Emmitt knew the catch, though. Rory was a product of good parenting. Huff and Annmarie Larsen loved unconditionally, perhaps, but they brooked no nonsense. Emmitt doubted that as a father he could do the same. Not that he'd ever seen himself in that situation. A variety of reasons existed for this—though in truth only one and a reason he rarely chose to ponder. Usually only when he was very drunk, things weren't going his way, and he needed someone to blame.

"How's your mother, Rory?"

"Oh, you know, Mr. Emmitt. She's still angry at Dad going off and dying like he did."

A sudden silence fell across the room as Rory, eyes at the floor, shuffled back on forth on his feet for a minute before looking back up at Emmitt.

"Damn. I'm sorry, Mr. Emmitt."

"Nothing to be sorry for." He meant it. "That's what people do, Rory," he said. "After awhile they die. But I can see how your mom would be angry. It was a foolish thing, what your dad did."

"Well, yeah. I mean, it hurts me, too. You know?"

"I do."

"I guess you do." Rory hesitated, his eyes back staring at the floor for a minute before he continued. "I was really sorry to hear about Mrs. Raines. Mom, too. I hope you know that."

"Yes. And thank you. Thank your mom for me, too. If I don't get to see her this trip."

"I will." He was quiet for a minute, moved toward the door as if to leave, but stopped.

"That was just like Dad," he said. A friend of his wants to go offshore in his new boat 'cause there's an amazing tuna run going down, and he was going. Didn't matter if the weather people said an out of season Nor'easter was barreling down right where he was headed. Or that Mom pitched a major fit, yelling and screaming how he was a damn fool. And when that didn't work, begged him not to go."

Rory had been staring out the window at the harbor while he spoke. When he turned back to Emmitt there was a goofy grin on his freckled face.

"And Mom begging the old man, Mr. Emmitt? Now that's something I thought I'd never see."

"No," Emmitt said, "you're right about that. It doesn't seem possible."

Beyond the windows it was quiet on the streets of Ferry Town, other than the occasional boat horn. Tourist season on the island ended abruptly right after Labor Day and the summer throngs were gone. He had been on the island once in the summer. He hadn't liked it. The swarm of humans in cars, or on foot, had seemed suffocating to Emmitt.

Besides, the fishing was better in the fall. With a rush of sadness, he realized how much he missed his old fishing partner, Huff.

"It was weird, Mr. Emmitt," Rory said. "But when Mom heard about what happened to Dad out on the Banks, for a moment there was a look on her face. Sort of like, 'See? I told you!' It didn't last long, though."

"I imagine not." He knew there could have been no vindication for Huff's widow. And said again, "No, I imagine not.

***

Why Emmitt thought of the first time Dana had ever been angry with him, he wasn't sure. Certainly, being on Squanocket—a place where he and Dana had been very happy—had something to do with it. And maybe it was something even simpler: the fact it was raining hard outside. Like it had been that afternoon, when he came into the house with the mail.

They had been married close to a year, living in a one bedroom apartment down from the courthouse. His book was selling okay, just not enough to afford them all that he wanted to provide for his new wife. As Dana reminded him when he was being hard on himself, he was still young, it was his first book, the reviews had been decent, she had a good job with the school district, everything was fine, and she was happy, happier than she had ever been in her life. There was all the time in the world stretching out in front of them. The next book would be even better. Everything they dreamed of was still to come. And besides, she liked to add, her grin lighting up the freckled features of her face, money or not, his book had led him to her. Surely that was enough. Wasn't it Emmitt?

None of which he could argue with, even if he wanted to. Her belief was strong enough for the two of them. Especially at those times when he had none of his own.

But it was raining very hard that afternoon, one of those late summer deluges common in the months of August and September. Though they were barely into September, Emmitt reassured himself with the fact that October would come soon. The weather would clear out, be again that fresh cool clean time of year when everything seemed fine and worthy of being alive for. With a little luck he might have finished the first draft of the book he was working on—and that was giving him fits. If that were the case, perhaps they would have enough money set aside to go down to the Keys. Do some long overdue fishing and diving. The cooling water, and what lay beneath it, would be a fitting reward after the long, hot and dreary months of a summer in Florida.

The letter slipped out of the stack of bills and junk mail as he went to place them on his desk. The envelope was one of those airmail ones, with the red and blue borders, Airmail written on one side, and Aero mail on the other, that Emmitt had always found fascinating and exotic as a child, thinking when one came for his mother that it must carry news from some far off land. If not for the return address, though, he would have put it off to the side and done his best to get through the bills first. But the words, *Ms. Eileen Hobart* on the top line of the return address slot—written in a very neat feminine hand that even after three years Emmitt recognized—got his attention immediately.

As did the contents of the letter. For according to Eileen, and unbeknownst to him, Emmitt was a father. Not with Eileen. But with Anna. His daughter was a bright, lovely little girl, three years old and named Emily. Emily Hobart. And not Raines after her father. But that wasn't the worst of what the letter contained. Not at all. For it seemed that Anna had suddenly disappeared, gone now for almost two weeks, and where she was going no one knew. Eileen wrote not only to tell Emmitt about his child, but also to warn him. Anna was volatile—as she was sure he remembered. It was certainly possible she might show up looking for him. If she wasn't strung out somewhere. Or dead. But if she did show up at his place, then please be kind, try to get her some help, or at least put her on a bus back to West Virginia.

Stunned and in need of a drink, Emmitt left it on the desk, unfortunately, right where Dana was able to find it when she came home from work.

"Who's Eileen Hobart?"

"I told you about her."

He was sitting at the coffee table in the living room, just finished with his drink and debating the merits of another one, when Dana came in, envelope in one hand. He hated the idea of being suddenly on the defensive. Especially when he didn't think he should be. He was also glad it was only the envelope she was holding. She hadn't read the letter. He didn't think the Dana he knew would do such a thing. He wanted to be the one to tell her what the letter said—didn't want her to find it out on her own.

"Is this something I should be worried about?"

"That's hard to say. I don't know myself if I should be worried."

"Well Jesus, Emmitt, you've got to tell me something."

She sat down on the other end of the couch. His mother had given them the sofa for a housewarming gift and Dana had never particularly liked it. She claimed it was too big for the small apartment and that the color was all wrong. The fact she had to sit there now to find out what the letter and Eileen were all about—judging by the screwed tight frown on her face—wasn't helping anything.

"You're drinking already," she said, pointing with the envelope at his empty cocktail glass. "Do I need a drink?"

"Probably wouldn't hurt." Seeing she wasn't buying into his attempt to lighten the mood, he added quickly, "Better let me get you a glass of wine."

Was the news within the letter that terrible? Dana's reaction, the hard tone in her voice, when he told her certainly made it seem that way.

"You have a child with her?"

"Well no, not with her. With her sister. Anna."

"Her sister? You talked some about Eileen. How she left you suddenly. But her sister? I don't remember that."

"I probably never told you. Didn't want you to think bad of me. Besides, it's long over and done with. Or so I thought."

"So you were just never going to tell me? That you got Eileen's sister pregnant?"

"Goddamn, Dana! This is the first I heard."

Whether she didn't believe him, or didn't want to believe him, Emmitt didn't know. Nor did he find out right then, for Dana got up and left the room, went into the bedroom, and shut the door. Fearing the quiet coming from there, and standing it until he couldn't anymore,

Emmitt finally knocked on the door and asked if everything was all right, did she need anything?

"I need you to go away. Just leave me alone, Emmitt. For now. Please."

He couldn't think of anywhere to go. Other than to make another drink and sit on the couch and see how long it took for his life to get back to normal. When he woke up the next morning he was still on the sofa. Apparently it was going to take longer for normal to return than he had first thought.

Over coffee in the kitchen alcove that served as the dining room for the apartment, Emmitt brought up this new reality Eileen's letter had delivered.

"I better go."

"West Virginia?" Red-eyed, and sullen, Dana's reddish blonde hair hung in a mess around her face. "To meet your child?"

"I think I should—don't you? I Know Eileen says it isn't necessary. That the child has everything she needs. So I guess it's up to me. But I think I should."

"Emily, huh? Pretty close to Emmitt. Seems this Anna Hobart cared enough for you to name your child after you."

"I hadn't thought of that."

"You can be damn dense at times, Em." For a moment her anger looked ready to flare up again. Fortunately it didn't. There was only that sullen sort of sadness when she spoke again. "One of the many reasons I love you, I suppose. We could both go, you know. To meet your daughter."

"I was hoping you'd want to," he said as he refilled their coffee.

"Want might not be the right word. But I would. You decide."

"I want you to come with me."

They were both silent for a while in the dim light of the kitchen. The Venetian blinds over the one little window above the table were closed, even though the sun was fully up outside. But the darkness of inside had suited his mood better and he chose to leave it that way. Dana must have felt the same for she did nothing to change it.

"What about the mother, Em? Anna. Do you think she's going to turn up here? I don't know if I could handle that."

"Anna Hobart's a junkie, Dana. Last time I saw her she was leaving to go score with a friend of hers. Two days later I was told she'd OD'd. That's the last I saw of her. Last I saw of Eileen. I suppose anything is possible with Anna, but my guess is that she's probably off somewhere doing her thing."

"Jesus. That poor kid."

"Eileen will take good care of her. The grandparents, too, I'm sure."

Again it was quiet between them—a quiet broken only by the sounds of traffic outside, their neighbors leaving for work or perhaps to take their children to school, until Emmitt thought of something.

"Christ, the Hobart family owns half the coal in West Virginia. Probably a good chunk of what's in Kentucky, too." His coffee had gone cold and after refilling his cup and Dana's he continued. "Still, she's my kid. I need to help."

"I wouldn't think much of you, Em, if you didn't. But I think the question of child support is up to the courts." She frowned for a second. "If Eileen is reaching out to you now about the child then I imagine she has a plan for what comes next."

"Eileen is not the vindictive type, if that's what you're thinking. She's not going to take me to the cleaners over money for the kid. I'll write her after breakfast and see when a good time to come is. We'll take it from there."

***

The answer he received from Eileen, as much as he hated to think so, was a relief. Now, was not a good time to come, Eileen wrote back. Her mother had just died. Thankfully, Anna had returned and was in rehab again. Their father wasn't handling either of these too well. As for child support, she would talk to the family attorney about it and see what he suggested. It was reassuring, though, that he brought it up. She would let him know as soon as she knew.

He answered her with a brief letter expressing how sorry he was for the loss of her mother and for Anna being in a rehab. He wished all of them well and when it was okay to come just let him know. He put a check for two hundred in the envelope with the letter and sent it off.

The money was for now, he added in a post script. Until he heard from her attorney and everything was set up.

To his surprise, instead of right away, he didn't hear back from Eileen until Christmas. This time it was a card, along with a photograph of a little girl. She had her mother's fine blonde hair and blue eyes. Emmitt could see some of him in her, if only in the set of her face, a tight little smile on her lips, similar to the one he put on for the camera in the photos of him as a child his mother kept in an album she liked to bring out around the holidays.

For reasons he couldn't explain Emmitt didn't show this card to Dana. Nor did he write back—other than to send the monthly check. He threw the card away, but kept the photograph, tucking it away in the desk drawer where he kept other papers. Ones he rarely looked at, but was afraid to get rid of.

And that was how they left it, Dana and him. After some time, the normal he had been waiting on that night on the couch while Dana was sobbing in their bedroom with the door closed, did return. Other than casually, Eileen, Anna, the child, rarely came up.

Until four years later—after Dana's first miscarriage.

"At least you have a child." Weak as she was and looking damn near dead, Dana's words coming at him from the hospital bed still cut him to the core.

"Jesus, baby, that's the last thing on my mind right now."

"Is it?"

"God yes. I'm only wanting you to get better and when you're ready we can try again. I love you, baby. I love you."

Now, in bed in the loft above the bike shop on his first night on the island, Emmitt hated how these were the memories that came to him. Bad ones from the past that had nothing even to do with where he was. When he should be thinking, if anything, about the many good times he'd spent there with Dana. Rolling over to face the wall, the pillow clutched tight beneath his head, Emmitt relaxed a little and tried to put everything out of his mind. Sleep didn't come easy and took a long time.

Part One: New River

It wasn't any urgent need that drove him to Anna's room that night. Not when everything he could possibly want, or need from a woman was offered freely to him by Eileen. A woman who knew Emmitt was going to her sister's bedroom when he left her bed, even giving him a sleepy smile before leaving their room. Her acceptance of this situation something Emmitt didn't quite understand.

So, because he could, Emmitt walked down the hall just the same.

"Uh oh," Anna said. "Something wrong?"

"No. Eileen had a rough day at work and is beat is all."

"And you're not?"

"Not what?"

"Beat?"

"No."

By then he was naked and next to her on the sheets she had thrown back when he came into her room, her pale naked body soft and waiting in the weak light of the moonlight coming through the open window.

"Yeah?"

She ran a hand along his chest, fingers stopping at one nipple to rub it lightly between them. He knew what was coming next, having learned from the beginning of whatever it was he had with this other sister, that Anna was uninhibited in bed, to the point of sometimes being a little rough. So when she leaned over and took the nipple she had been teasing with her fingers and bit it he was not surprised.

"You know what I think, Emmit?"

"About what?" he asked, his mind elsewhere.

"That it's a good thing, yes?" The sardonic smile he knew so well from her, was all over her face when she looked up from his chest and into his eyes. The fingers tracing along his skin, were now holding his penis—which like his nipple, had hardened with her touch. "There's two of us for you?" she teased.

"Yeah." He rolled over and into her. "A very good thing."

And for quite a while it *was* a good thing, and in the bright light of the summer days seeming to roll on and on, Emmitt Raines could almost believe it was okay, quite normal in fact. He was young, twenty four, and working on what he hoped to be his first novel. His day job, at the bike rental shop on the beach, paid his bills, even leaving a little extra for fun stuff. But his work at the bike shop on the beach, along with the steady sound of the surf rolling in, made him feel that his mundane job wasn't so mundane after all. And with the writing he did at night, hell, he deserved two women in his life. His former roommates out of the picture—Bosco dead and Croc in jail for who knew how long—he would have been lonely had he stayed on in the house they shared. Not that staying there was an option. Good job or not he could never have afforded it on his own.

So when Eileen, a girl Bosco had introduced Emmitt to and that he had been seeing ever since, suggested he move in with her at her place on the New River, he had quickly agreed. He loved her, after all. Or at least he was pretty sure he did. Her offer was certainly a better one than his only other option—that of moving back home with his mother.

It was the first time Emmitt had ever lived with a woman he was involved with, and it took some getting used to. It was certainly different from living with his best friends at the house off the causeway to the beach. For one thing it was much cleaner. The kitchen sink wasn't stacked with dirty dishes, empty beer cans didn't litter the coffee table in the living room, and the ashtrays scattered around the place weren't full to overflowing. It was quieter as well, his new quarters empty of the loud music Bosco put on the stereo first thing in the morning, and stayed on until whoever was last to hit the rack at night thought to turn it off.

Emmitt quickly found that he took to the new living scene quickly, enjoying a peace he hadn't known since leaving his mother's house for college and dorm life five years before.

Besides Eileen and the clean gend quiet surroundings, there was one other factor of living in the house across from the river—and that was the river itself. On nights when Eileen was busy working on one of her visual arts projects, and Emmitt at a standstill with his writing, to get away from it he liked to grab up the spinning rod his grandfather had given him years before. Taking the canvas bag of lures—also courtesy of his grandfather—he would go across the street to the dock edging out into the river. The fishing was best when the tide was outgoing but good tide or not, he still liked to go.

There, with the street behind him mostly quiet, Emmitt would see a light glowing softly against the night where Eileen was cozy inside. Emmitt would cast big topwater bomber plugs into the flowing water, twitching it until he was rewarded with the crashing bang of a big snook taking the bait, or sometimes just a lowly jack crevalle. And not often, but it did happen, the explosion of a tarpon, a big silver king, rushed the plug, inhaling it and running with it until it broke him off, because there was no way Emmitt could ever hope to stop the run of a fish like that.

And sometimes nothing struck the plug, no predator of the deep interested in whatever lure he dug out of the canvas bag and cast out into the night. And that was okay, too. For after these nocturnal trips across the street to test his luck on the water, he felt refreshed. Felt new. Felt like everything in his life was just fine.

And for a while it was all he could ask for. A good woman, who loved him and that he loved in return. A cool old house down by the river where at night the two of them could get high, listen to music on the stereo, and make love with the windows open and to the sounds music, the wind outside sighing through the seagrape trees, and the boats moving up and down New River in the night. Yes, it was certainly a good way to pass the time until he decided to do whatever he was going to do next with his life.

But then Anna appeared. The sister Eileen had only casually mentioned when he asked about her family. Eileen had described how she was estranged from her parents. Neither her father—a wealthy coal mine owner in West Virginia where she had grown up—or her mother approved of what they called the worthless hippie life their daughter chose to live. As for Anna, her sister, Eileen said that she showed up in her life off and on, more off than on, and usually when she was trying to kick the heroin habit she had picked up at Stonybrook where she went to college.

So that when Anna appeared at the house on New River, skinny, shaking, ragged looking, asking her sister if Eileen would give her one more chance. Eileen had no choice, and Emmitt couldn't say no when Eileen said yes.

Even then it was all okay and normal. Or as normal as anything else was at the time. Until the Friday afternoon a few months back when after she came home from work, Eileen had told him that she was going up to Cocoa Beach for the weekend to see an old girlfriend she hadn't seen in years and who had tracked her down. Did he mind keeping an eye on Anna, who was doing better? Last Tango in Paris, the new Brando film was playing downtown. Maybe he could take her to see it. She had mentioned just the other day she wanted to.

Emmitt didn't want to—in fact he felt uncomfortable around Anna, who had a habit of walking around the house in the morning wearing just her panties while both Emmitt and Eileen were getting ready to go to their respective jobs. But he had said yes. He pretty much regretted that decision ever since. After the movie they had stopped in at the bar next door to the theater. From there, and maybe because of the movie and the sex scenes that had indeed aroused them, when they got back to the house they ended up in Anna's bed.

"Eileen will be pleased we did this," Anna had said in the morning.

"You're not going to tell her?"

"Of course I am. We tell each other everything."

Before he could protest, beg her not to, she had pulled him back into bed and they made love again.

Instead of everything blowing up and falling apart, to his amazement, Eileen only smiled when Anna told her what had happened.

"Cool," Eileen had said, and then kissed Emmitt. "Thank you for being nice to my sister."

Now, here he was, living with Eileen and Anna Hobart in the old house beneath the Seventh Avenue Bridge, where one or the other sisters were usually around. He would talk to, laugh with, make love with, or just hang out together listening to music while getting high on pot Bosco left behind and that appeared to have no bottom. The only one of the three who seemed to feel funny about the whole scene, or to suffer any guilt, seemed to be him—try as he might to let it go and take it for what it was.

Other than that there was a lot going on in the world and it was being shown on TV. Every evening at 6:30 there were endless film clips of the Vietnam conflict, the ravaged countryside and people, countless body bags of soldiers waiting on the tarmac to be flown home for burial Then there was President Nixon proclaiming the U.S. would not go into Laos or Cambodia after the VC, even while underground papers—the aboveground ones, as well—reported on how American troops were already deep inside both of those regions chasing down the "Communist threat." The Watergate story broke that summer, vague at first in the newspapers and broadcast news stations, growing more in depth as details came to light of the workings of C.R.E.E.P, Nixon's re-election committee.

Even though he wore his black hair long and liked to smoke pot, adhered to the politics of make love, not war, Emmitt never considered himself a hippie. He just tried to go with the flow. But between the war, the president, the protestors raging in the streets to no apparent avail, it occurred to Emmitt that all the revolutionary promise of the decade before was either yet to come or was never going to.

"You know," Anna said one evening. The three of them were gathered in the living room watching Allen Ginsberg being interviewed about the ongoing state of unrest in America, "that's what's wrong with art in this country in the first place."

"What is, Anna?" Eileen was curled up next to Emmitt on the couch with a catalog of albums for potential ordering from the record store where she worked in her lap. She'd been browsing through it while half watching the interview.

"This whole thing with Ginsberg and other writers and painters going on and on about politics and all that horse shit." Anna sat in the tattered armchair across the room, the paint-splattered T-shirt she wore reflecting the various colors in the flickering gray light of the TV screen. "Man," she went on, "the news of the world and what it means are for the reporters and the editorial hacks and not the artists, Eileen. You should know that."

"Oh, I do, Anna. Yes, I do."

Emmitt saw Eileen's version of the Hobart sardonic smile flicker across her face. If the sisters were quite different in looks—Eileen being somewhat Rubenesque and with short curly brown hair that hung around her face in ringlets much like one of those girls in the old time Coca-Cola ads, and Anna was taller, leaner, with straight blonde hair down past her shoulders, but they still shared that smile.

"I just can't find it in myself anymore," Eileen continued, "to get worked up about that sort of stuff."

"Well, if *you* can't, Emmitt should be. He's a freaking artist himself, after all. Man, anyone into searching for, creating truth, man, they have to be. 'All that sort of stuff,' as you put it, Eileen, takes the truth out of poetry and painting. News of the world is a domain any real artist would stay far, far away from if he is serious about transcendence. Otherwise it all disappears and we're fucked."

He took good notice of Anna's hard tone, the serious set of her face, along with the disgust, not to mention sadness, in her last statement. He hadn't put much thought into the current events of the world's place in anything he was writing. His stories so far concerned events of the past. He'd never really thought about Anna's commitment to *her* work, as far as that went, the passion and ideas behind what she put on canvas. He admired the landscapes she created, the soft, surreal portraits she had painted of Eileen, and him, both together, and separate; paintings she had framed and then hung on the walls of the living room.

There was a fourth painting, just finished and put up in the hallway. It was of a girl, long blonde hair falling around her shoulders, back turned to the viewer so that her face, staring out a window, visible over one shoulder, could not be seen. Beyond the window a shimmering mass of pale blue color flowed away from the girl. Anna called the painting, "Self Portrait,' a title Eileen thought horrible. Emmitt liked the painting; liked it a lot, related, in fact, to it more than he wished he did.

"What you're saying makes sense, Anna," he said now, uncoiling from Eileen's easy-going embrace to reach for the wine bottle on the coffee table. "I've never been a big fan of Ginsberg's stuff anyways. Kind'a think he's more of a sham, or a showman, than serious poet. For myself, though, and any story I'm working on—well, I guess the idea of putting a *message* into it, or thinking I'm going to change the world with what I write, that's never been much of it. I'd just like to capture the feel of what I'm writing—do my best to get a good picture of the people involved and what happened. Even if I know I've got a damn long way to go yet before I'm any good at it."

"You sell yourself short, Emmitt," Eileen said as she took the wine from him. "But I think both of you are wrong. And right. Look at Emile Zola. Goya's paintings of war and the Inquisition in Spain. Or Sinclair Lewis. Harriet Beecher Stowe."

"You certainly can't call Harriet Beecher Stowe much of an artist." Anna laughed when it was her turn with the wine. "I mean, seriously. Have either of you read 'Uncle Tom's Cabin'? Yes, it got the ball rolling big time on that whole slavery thing that led to the Civil War. And eventually to King and the other black leaders of today. Still, it's just a cheap thriller if you ask me."

Emmitt had leafed through an old, hardbound copy of the book as a kid of ten or so, the binders still barely holding the yellowing pages together. He'd been unable to get into the writing style, but still thoroughly enjoyed the woodcuts of Little Eva, Simon Legree, the poor old darkies slaving on the plantation beneath the overseer's lash, and such. The book had been given to his mother by her great-grandmother, who in turn, when she, too, was just a young girl and living in Atlanta in the days after Sherman's troops came through, had been given the book by some nameless aunt. Emmitt's great-great grandmother had inscribed on the fly-leaf the story of when Lincoln met Mrs. Stowe and said to her, "So you're the little lady that's started all this trouble." The inscription ended with a postscript of, "And didn't she, though!" and the date of the gift: Christmas, 1935.

"I *did* read it," Eileen said. "A little archaic, I guess, but a good story just the same."

"My point exactly," Anna snorted. "There's a difference between 'stories' and serious art. That particular tale was written by a woman who'd never been south of the Mason/Dixon Line, never been on a plantation, had no intimate knowledge of what she was writing about. Which proves my point: artists should stick to the truth, and beauty, like Keats wrote of so finely. Leave the rabble-rousing to the soulless ones."

Emmitt could see how the debate was an endless one, regardless of Anna—as she claimed—"proving her point." More importantly was this first glimpse of how Anna Hobart was more than just a girl he got high with, hung out with, and had sex with on occasion when her sister wasn't around, or just didn't feel like it, and he running with the energy of his age, did. What was he going to do with this newfound knowledge? He wasn't sure. Somehow this bothered him.

Until later that night, laying spoon fashion with Eileen in the bedroom they shared, he decided Anna wasn't his problem.

But on a morning in late August, when he was sitting on the front porch with a cup of coffee, watching the river across the street had been flowing for years before the white men arrived in Ft. Lauderdale, pushed the Indians out, and created the city Emmitt came to grow up in—Anna became his problem.

The final pages of the manuscript he'd been working on the last three years were on the table in front of him as he watched the morning unfold, the river and the light filtering through the seagrape trees overhanging the water. He was proud of himself for having reached the finish line of his work, though he realized there was a lot of rewriting ahead. Yet, the bulk of it was done, the hard part, the first go round. He had done that. Now it was on to the next part. It had been a good summer, if strange, this life he had with the Hobart sisters. But it was what he had. Not knowing what else to do, he had gone along. And Jesus, it wasn't too bad.

"Anna's in love with you. Just in case you didn't know."

Somehow Eileen was *just* there, standing behind him, hands suddenly resting on his shoulders, voice soft and low in his ear.

"I never thought it would get that far, Emmitt and that's on me. I just wanted her to have a connection with another human being besides me. I thought it would help her. You were there, I thought I could handle it, thought both you and her could handle it. But I was wrong, Emmitt. Way wrong."

He started to say something, but she stopped him.

"Now, here's the thing. What are we going to do about it? I don't know and I bet you don't either. So we will have to figure it out. Together."

He was grateful for the 'we' in her question. And the 'together' part. As for the rest of it? For the moment that was beyond Emmitt's grasp.

***

The solution to the problem arrived in an unexpected way. A party. This wasn't Emmitt's idea, but coming so soon on the heels of Eileen's morning bombshell he was glad for the diversion. Labor Day and the end of summer was as good an excuse for a blow-out as anything else, he figured.

Anna brought the idea up one night when she barged into the bedroom where Emmitt had just taken Eileen into his arms.

"Anna!" Eileen laughed when her sister burst into the room. "What about knocking first, you maniac."

"I'm way too excited to bother with that," Anna said, her voice louder than it needed to be in the small room. She'd been out that night and it was plain, even in the dim light of the bedroom, that she was very high. "I've had the brainstorm of the year, the perfect way to liven up this freakin' morgue we've been living in lately. We're throwing a party! Music, dope and wine. And yes! I am a maniac."

Lately, Anna had been hanging out with old girlfriends from school she'd looked up and were still in town. She'd been going out with a guy, as well, also from her past. Emmitt was curious about this but had said nothing until one afternoon when he came in from work. Expecting both sisters to be home, he was surprised to find only Eileen sitting on the edge of the bed in their room. It looked to him like she'd been crying.

"Jesus, Eileen," he said, taking her in his arms. "What's wrong?"

"Anna, I guess. Though there's no guessing about it, actually."

"Ah. Okay. What'd she do now?"

"I don't know that she's done anything. But she's with Lee right now. Has been going out with him, it seems."

"So, why the look? Maybe a boyfriend would be good for her."

The expression on her face reminded him of the morning on the porch when she had given him the news about Anna's feelings for him.

"Not this one. Lee can be trouble," Eileen said. "For Anna, anyways. And I guess whoever else gets in his path if they're not careful. She's come a long way in the last few months. I'd hate to see that get away from her."

"She used to do dope with him, I take it."

"Yes."

It was quiet in the room for a while, the afternoon light fading, the shadows inside the room beginning to cover everything in gray. Emmitt was thinking how nice it might be if both he and Eileen could be lost for just a little while in that gray.

"Yes," Eileen repeated. "She used to shoot dope with him. We both knew Lee from high school. His folks, like ours, had money and were away a lot. Lee used to have kids over to their house when they were gone, everyone smoking pot and dropping acid. He and Anna went together for a long time, and it was great at first. He taught her how to surf and they spent a lot of time in the water and in the sun, taking weekend trips to different beaches up and down the east coast. I can't remember when she was so happy. I haven't seen her happy like that, since."

She pulled away from his arms and sat up straighter on the bed, wiping her eyes with the hem of the long dress she was wearing. In the half light of the afternoon fading in the room, Eileen seemed to fade as well, away from him, and into that gray.

"One of Lee's surfer pals he'd been doing acid with turned him onto heroin. It wasn't long before, in turn, Lee shared it with Anna. The outcome of this, after a year or so and while I was off with Tom in the wilds of Vermont, was my folks sending Anna to a hospital in Boston where she was able to get clean. After her release my father pulled some strings, and she was accepted into Emerson's art school. She stayed in Boston working on her degree. Stayed clean, too, for a while. I heard that Lee managed to get clean. Finally. That he ended up out in San Diego with some friends, just hanging out and doing a lot of surfing. Then his parents were killed in a car crash, and he came into more money than is good for someone like him. From what Anna tells me, he lives on a boat. He has it tied up at a slip in the Bahia Mar and spends his days fishing and surfing."

"Is he back shooting junk," Emmitt asked, "or whatever it is they do with it?"

"I don't know," Eileen leaned forward into his chest, laying her still wet face against his cheek. "I don't think Anna is and I can usually tell with her. I haven't seen Lee, so I don't know about him. But I don't like it."

"Yeah, I guess not."

He didn't like it either, though for reasons he hated to admit, even to himself.

Anna was right about one thing: it had been like a morgue inside the house under the bridge. The three of them, since Eileen's newsflash for Emmitt, walked around one another like on eggshells. Eileen went to her parents in Palm Beach and Emmitt worked hard at avoiding Anna. The first night as he lay alone in bed, he tried not to think of her presence in the room just down the hall. He half hoped she'd come to him *this* time, absolving him of blame on his part for what would happen then. She didn't and eventually he fell asleep, not knowing if he was grateful she hadn't or disappointed.

"She said something to you." Anna cornered him in the hallway the next morning as he was coming out of the bathroom and late for work at the bike shop. "Eileen told you. Didn't she?"

"Yeah, she said something." He went to move around her, suddenly more aware of her nakedness under the thin cotton T-shirt than he wanted to be. "Can't we talk about this later? Jay's been on my ass all week as it is. If bike rentals don't pick up soon I may be out of a freaking job."

She laughed at the hang dog look he knew was on his face.

"Well then, Emmitt, baby, run along if that's what you have to do. But don't sweat it so. Your job, and me, and how I may, or may not, feel. Besides, it's not like you can hurt me, anyways."

The way her blonde eyebrows drew close together above those so very blue eyes, the hard set of her lips, made him wonder if this were true.

"Geez, lover boy." She laughed again, the laugh hard and strained. "Ease up a little. That frown on your face doesn't look good on you. Man, it's not like we're going to ask you to pick one of us over the other. But if you're that confused about it, maybe I'll back off."

She leaned in suddenly, pushing him back against the wall with her hands on his bare chest, her groin against his as she kissed him hard, her tongue thrusting into his mouth.

"Is that what you want?" Just as suddenly she pulled away from him. "For me to back off?"

He didn't know. He knew only that right then he wanted to kiss her again—wanted to feel that hot body pressed into his. But she had pulled away completely, leaning back against the wall in the narrow hallway, that Hobart smile stretching her thin lips.

"You're cute when you're confused," she laughed, and was gone. The erection she left him with didn't go down completely until the morning was almost over.

***

All that day at work customers came and went steadily in the bike shop, the Strip running along A1A and the beach, thronging with more cars and people than had been present for some time.. He was aware of the bright August sunlight beating down on the beach on the other side of the highway—of how that light seemed to stretch on forever while he went about the motions of working: finding the bikes the customers wanted to rent, writing up slips, adjusting seats, getting the customers out of the store and back on the street. Mainly he tried to stay out of the boss' way. Even with the unexpected crush of customers, Jay was still in a foul humor about something. He sat by himself near the bike repair stand in the back of the room, looking at the newspaper, chain-smoking cigarettes, and glancing up with a scowl whenever the trip alarm went off as a customer came into the shop.

As he went about the motions of work Emmitt kept asking himself over and over again what he wanted—if anything. But Anna was correct: cute, or not, he was definitely confused.

***

Labor Day weekend came along with the "End of Summer" party. While Emmitt did what he could to help, the two sisters spent most of the week preceding the party decorating. Anna slapped together some poster art, using pastels to create Impressionistic images of beach scenes, kids catching the first school bus of the fall, empty playgrounds and such that Emmitt thought were definitely deserving of more than just the short party life they were designed for. Eileen made collages of her own, out of photographs taken from of surfing magazines: pictures of girls and boys leaving the beaches with surfboards under their arms or sitting forlornly on the sand in the late afternoon, knees drawn up to their chest as dusk fell and the waves went flat with the ceasing of the day's winds and tide. They hung the posters throughout the house, while in the yard, at the directions of the two sisters, Emmitt strung Chinese lanterns along the edge of the back porch and in the branches of the oak and sea grape trees.

These were all good efforts at decorating Emmitt thought, but the night of the party he wondered at one point if anyone even noticed. The crush of people was more than Eileen and Anna expected but they were delighted with it all the same. Most of the party crowd stayed out in the backyard where Emmitt had set up a keg of beer. The night was a hot and sticky, even with a breeze off the river. Between the heat and the festive mood the keg stayed very busy.

Some guys who worked at the record shop with Eileen arranged their amps under the sea grape trees and ran long extension cords into the house. As night fell on that Saturday evening the sounds of electric guitars being tuned rose out of the backyard. People stood on the grass or leaned up against the fence by the impromptu stage, plastic cups of frothy beer in hand while the makeshift band ran through a series of old Beach Boys tunes, early Beatles songs, and a smattering of Rolling Stones. The whole scene was lit by the paper lanterns swaying in the light evening breeze sifting through the yard.

Other than the guys from the record shop, Emmitt knew very few of the party goers flowing in and out. While Eileen and Anna moved among the throng smiling and talking and with wine glasses full of a merlot, he hung back. He'd started off the party with the cold beer from the keg. But by the time night came on fully he decided he needed something with a little more kick. This decision was fueled partly because he just wanted to but mainly it was because he was uncomfortable with the mass of strangers crowding the house and yard. With Eileen mingling with friends from school and elsewhere, her sister doing the same, Emmitt suddenly felt very alone. He wished Bosco and Croc were around, pals of his own that he could talk and laugh with. That wasn't possible—leaving whiskey to fill the void.

Luckily for him a bottle of sour mash he had bought on a whim a few weeks back was still under the sink in the kitchen. Tossing his empty cup into one of the garbage containers placed by the back steps, he went inside to retrieve it. The first whiskey and ice he made went down quickly. Liking the pleasant glow soothing over his senses he made another. Taking it along with him he headed for the bathroom to relieve himself of the beer he'd begun the night with. Washing his hands afterwards he looked up and saw his face in the mirror staring back at him. The dark haired features in the glass shrugged.

As the party flowed on with steady drinks of the whiskey, Emmitt felt more and more adrift again. He decided to find Eileen. That would help. He found Anna, instead, and wished he hadn't.

She was in the kitchen in a corner by the refrigerator, arms wrapped around some guy, the two of them oblivious to anything around other than the kiss they were involved with.

"Hey, Emmitt," Anna said, pulling away from her partner when Emmitt coughed. Her partner was tall, over six feet Emmitt figured, with a blond prep school sort of look. A light turtleneck sweater covered his lanky torso, faded corduroy jeans slung casually off his hips. Like the rest of him his face was thin and pale in the harsh light of the kitchen.

"This is my good friend, Lee," Anna went on, tugging at the cotton blouse that had ridden up on her stomach in the heat of the kiss. "I don't think you've met him before."

In the stark light of the room Emmitt saw her eyes were soft and dilated.

"No, I haven't." Lee went to shake hands, but Emmitt backed away, opening the cabinet beneath the sink to pull out the bottle of bourbon he'd left there. "But I've heard a lot about him."

"All of it good?" Lee was still holding onto Anna's waist, the hand he had offered to Emmitt hanging loosely now at his side.

"Not really."

"Yeah, well, I get that a lot. I've been working hard at accepting it as my fate." He smiled wanly. "We all have our crosses to bear."

"If you say so."

"Emmitt," Anna said. "If you're looking for Eileen she went with Dwayne and Sherry to get more wine. And ice. Told me to tell you if I saw you that she had to go out and would be back soon."

"Okay." He was suddenly angry, rather than feeling adrift. "All right. I won't bother looking anymore."

Finished refilling his glass with ice and bourbon, he grabbed the bottle and headed for the living room.

"What do I tell Eileen when she gets back? Emmitt, man? Where you are?" Anna called out after him.

"Tell her I'm on the dock across the street," he said over his shoulder. "Tell her I needed some fresh air. That ought to cover it."

The night was still warm and sticky when he stepped out of the front door. Maybe even more so now that the breezes of earlier had died down. Midnight, and the end of the day, wasn't far off. Less than an hour, he thought when he closed the door behind him. He crossed the street over to the banks of where the river—a big oxbow that flowed behind the house, under the bridge, and around—continued its way to the Atlantic. Everything along the street was quiet and still—other than the noise of the party behind him. He took a deep breath of the humid night air, the smell of the falling tide almost a taste in his mouth. He sat down on the dock still holding onto the bottle of whisky and the water glass, the ice inside the glass melting in the warm September night.

The wood of the dock was hard beneath his buttocks as he lifted the glass of whiskey to his lips and drained it. The thought of the two sisters, of how he had been with them, the three of them high, happy, and in love, became a steady noise inside his head.

He wondered if he loved them both or if he really didn't love either one of them.

"Emmitt?" Like that morning on the back porch, out of nowhere Eileen was there, crouching down behind him on the dock, hands soft on his shoulders, voice low in his ear as she repeated, "Emmitt?"

"Yes, baby, 'tis I. Your one and only." If the words had sounded cavalier-like in his brain before he spoke, he was surprised how they came out slightly slurred.

"I was worried about you." Wrapping her arms tight around him she hugged him, her breath against his neck warm and soothing like the breeze, welcoming and just starting to lift off the river, he thought. "I came back from the store, babe but you were gone. I asked Anna if she knew where you were, and she said you'd left."

"I told her I'd be here." He waved at the river in front of them. "It's as far as I could go without making a swim for it." His laugh sounded hollow to him. Drunk and hollow, he thought. "Doesn't seem like a bad idea, come to think of it."

"I'd miss you if you weren't here."

She hugged him even tighter, kissing his neck lightly, Emmitt vaguely aware of the pressure of her breasts against his back, her soft hair brushing along his skin.

"Seems like I've got to go somewhere."

He pulled away, the sudden truth of what he'd just said laid out in the night air plain for him to see.

"Is that what you really think?"

With an easy pressure of her hands she turned him around so that they faced one another. He missed the soothing of her breath against his neck—thought as he looked into her eyes, Jesus, she's so damn beautiful. Why would I go anywhere she wouldn't be?

"You think it's time to leave, Emmitt? Because of what's been going on with the three of us?"

"Yeah" he said. "There's that all right." First time it's been said out loud, too, he thought, by any of the parties involved. Other than when Eileen deemed it necessary for him to know how her sister felt. Back when it was too late for any of it to be stopped.

"So tell me? Where you're thinking of going. 'Cause other than your writing, and the job at Jay's, you've just been drifting along here. That's what I see. Perhaps there's more? Something I don't know? You and I were connected once, completely. Not so much, now."

Eileen picked the whiskey bottle up from the dock and took a sip—something he'd never seen her do, drink hard liquor like that. She grimaced as the hot whiskey went down and he couldn't help but laugh.

"Well, at least I was able to make you laugh,' she said. "Tells me you're still here with me, I guess. I don't see how you can drink this stuff. Perhaps one has to acquire a taste for it?"

"Maybe." He took the bottle, tilting his head back and letting the whiskey wash down his gullet. "I like it. Took to it immediately."

She didn't find this as funny as he did, though, and they sat in silence for a while, both of them very much aware of what hung between them now in that silence.

"Do you like me as much as the whiskey?"

He shook his head yes, seeing by the way she watched his hand reach for the bottle again it was best he leave it where it was.

"A lot of it's my fault, I know," she said after a bit. "I let things go when I could have prevented them from doing that."

"Goddamn right you could have prevented it. Telling me to take Anna to the movies that night? She's your sister for Christ's sake. Didn't you know what was going to happen? She's your sister. You must have known."

But his anger tasted as hollow as his slurred laugh had when Eileen first came out on the dock.

"You're right, Emmitt. I probably could have prevented everything. I wasn't thinking, I guess. But it's done now, and I can't change it. What I need to know is simple, though. What *do* you want? Now that things are what they are?"

Not knowing, he said nothing.

"Wouldn't you like to be whole again? Instead of this empty shell sitting out here like some kind of drunken fool and certainly nothing like the Emmitt Raines I've been in love with all this past year."

"Jesus, Eileen, what can I tell you?"

"Tell me what you want. That's all. Tell me that."

"I want you."

"Do you? I'm right here, you know." Wrapping her arms around him tightly again she said into his mouth as she leaned forward to kiss him. "I'm right here."

***

Boats continued their way up and down the river as the night wore on and Emmitt and Eileen made love, the two of them half dressed, using Emmitt's polo shirt as a blanket for Eileen to lay on against the hardness of the dock. The urgency that once ran strong between them was back. The familiar lust taking them away from everything, even the occasional car rolling by on the road behind their thrusting bodies, headlights not noticed and gone before either one of them could think that there *were* others out here. The sounds of laughter and music coming from the party still raging in the house across the street, washed over them as Emmitt entered her, the whole of her insides opening up for him, hot and sticky like the night air covering their naked skin. The whole mystery of it all was right there for him to feel, even drunk as he was, her needful thrusts matching his, the way it seemed so timeless and right and stretching beyond time. Into forever, maybe, whatever that might be. Not that he was thinking of it like that. He was simply inside of her, content at first to just rock slowly in and out, her breath gasping and hot on his neck. Content to stay like that until she wasn't. Until she moaned into his ear, "Now, Emmitt. Now really make love to me. Like you mean it."

When it was over and time returned for them both and they lay wrapped up together. His softening penis still inside of her, her legs around his back not letting him go, Eileen whispered into his ear one last time, "Now I know, Emmitt, God yes. I'm not the only one here. You're here with me, too. My worrying all for nothing and that you and I will always be."

***

When they went back to the house the party was still going strong. While Eileen headed off for the bathroom Emmitt leaned over the kitchen sink and splashed cool water on his face, trying to regain his bearings. The bright light overhead illuminated the old tile countertops and porcelain sink in a stark realness he wasn't exactly comfortable with at that moment.

"You found Eileen, I guess." He turned, to see Anna in the kitchen doorway, alone, blonde hair hanging wildly down her face, blue eyes lit up from the alcohol and whatever else she'd been doing. "Or she found you. Guess it doesn't matter either way. I can see that."

"Where's Lee?" he asked. "And yeah, she found me. I was out on the dock across the street."

"Lee had sudden business to take care of."

"Strange hour of the day for business."

"Strange business, I guess. I didn't ask him." Having apparently taken inventory of his condition, the wrinkled shirt, the wet hair pushed back from his forehead, she added, "Looks like it was pretty intense out there on the dock."

"You could say that." He softly pushed her away, not able to breathe it seemed, with her that close to him. "Me and you are going to stop what we've been doing."

"I thought we had. Judging by the way you left me alone the other night." The bitterness in her voice surprised him, even if a trace of it had been in every conversation they'd had of late. "Why is that Emmitt? Because of Eileen?"

"Because of Eileen." He felt almost sober now. "Exactly because of Eileen."

"I knew that was coming. My sister always finds a way to fuck up whatever good thing I've got going."

"You and I were 'good?'" The sex, yes, he thought. That was good. But what else? "I can't see it," he said. "Not with how I feel about Eileen."

"As usual, Emmitt, you're wrong. Sad thing is how you don't know it, yet. How you may never know it."

He heard the sound of Eileen coming out of the bathroom calling from the hallway for Emmitt, and then for Anna. At the sound of her name Anna vanished, gone it seemed to Emmitt, as suddenly as she had first appeared in the kitchen doorway with her accusations. Then Eileen was in his arms, asking, "Wasn't Anna just here?"

He supposed it was funny, in a strange sort of way—not that anything of late particularly was—but he wasn't able to answer her.

***

Eileen hadn't asked him to, and Anna said they wouldn't, but choose Emmitt did. Made that choice as Eileen and he lay gasping together on the dock after their frenzied union—the lonely wail from a boat's horn coming upriver sealing that decision with its pleading note. But it wasn't enough.

The next morning, when he was helping her get the house and yard in order again after the party, the phone rang. Eileen put the mop she was using on the kitchen floor back in the bucket and went to the phone hanging on the wall to answer it.

"What's wrong?"

He went ahead and asked, even knowing as he did by the expression on Eileen's face, the phone call had to do with Anna.

"That was my dad on the phone." She sounded the way she looked: pale and weak. "Anna's OD'd."

"Oh, Christ." He hesitated, not wanting to ask the next question, unable not to. "She's not dead is she? She's going to be okay, isn't she?"

"She's not dead, no. Lee is, but Anna was still breathing when the police got there. Thank God for that. But they don't know if she's going to be okay. The police called dad from Broward General where they took her. Him and mom are flying in from West Virginia this afternoon."

Wow, he thought as he went to take her in his arms. The hospital where I was born. So strange.

"I've got to get to the hospital." She swung out of his arms, one hand whipping the scarf from her hair as she crossed the living room to the bathroom in. "Anna needs me. My parents need me."

"Well hold on a minute and I'll go with you."

The coldness in her voice stopped him where he was.

"You can't. This is family business."

He was still standing in the kitchen doorway when she reappeared from the bedroom, house cleaning clothes replaced by a fresh blouse, peasant skirt and no-nonsense look on her face.

"I'll be back," she told him, stopping at the front door suddenly before turning the knob. "I don't know when. But as soon as I can."

Only, she never came back. She called once from the hospital, later that night. Anna was holding her own though it was still too early for the doctors to make any predictions. She said she would call him the next day. Told him she loved him, and then hung up, before he could say anything in return. Three days later, after the promised call never came, or any indication at all, as far as that went, Eileen still existed on the face of the planet, he went to the hospital.

"I'm sorry, sir," the receptionist at the front desk told him. Wide and airy as the information area of the hospital was, the harsh antiseptic smell of the facility rose freely into his senses, burning his nose and eyes. The smell of death, he decided. "You're not family. Without authorization I can't tell you the information you're asking for."

"Please" he pleaded. "Can't you tell me anything?" He was at the end, he realized. If he walked away from that place with nothing, nothing would be all he had. "Is Anna Hobart even still in this place?"

"Okay, okay, sir. But you have to settle down." Apparently the receptionist was going to take pity on him. "This is a hospital, you know. I'll tell you only this. Ms. Hobart was released yesterday morning. Where her family took her from here I'm not at liberty to say."

Slightly more than nothing, he thought, as the automatic glass doors sighed, slid open, and allowed him back into the land of the living. Not much, but something. Eileen would return soon. After she helped get her sister settled at the family home in West Virginia and back on her feet. Then she would come back to him. Thank God that Anna was still alive. Her sardonic smile, flashing blue eyes, the time she had danced on the sands of the beach behind the Yankee Clipper hotel, and swaying to music only she heard. The excited way she made love, her moans as she urged him deeper inside her body — these images flooding his mind as he looked for his Volkswagen in the parking lot of the hospital, the mid-day September sun streaming down and blinding him so that he had to shield his eyes against it to see properly.

He couldn't imagine Anna dead. Yet, it had been possible. Her boyfriend? That Lee guy? He was dead and they had both obviously shot up the same heroin. People died every day. Bosco evidence of that fact. Emmitt's father, too, on a lonely desperate night laying his head down on the tracks and waiting for the midnight northbound to end it all.

He found his car and wheeling out of the lot and onto Third Avenue he let that somber thinking go. Eileen would come back to the little house beneath the bridge. Just the two of them this time and it would be better that way. No distractions. None of that strange three-way relationship business that had brought them to this. He would work hard at making it all up to Eileen and it would be good again between them. The way it had been before Anna came knocking on the front door one early morning and everything changed.

He still thought it possible, three months later, on Christmas day with his mother, the two of them having their holiday meal in the house where he had grown up. All of it familiar, if different. Maybe because of the heavy gray in his mother's hair, now. Maybe because of the fact that he had changed over the years. Wasn't the same little boy who sat at that table when there was more family still alive for events such as these.

He still didn't understand how everything could have unraveled so quickly. Eating a quiet holiday meal with his mother at home he thought he still loved Eileen. And that it didn't seem to matter. She was gone. And everything over between them.

According to a Christmas card—one he found days after it had arrived lying in a bowl next to the Nativity scene on the dry sink— Eileen was sorry for how things had turned out. She certainly hadn't seen it coming. Hoped someday he would be able to forgive her

"I think of you often," she wrote, "and only with gladness in my heart. Love to you always Emmitt,

Eileen Hobart."

So yes, over Christmas dinner at his mother's house, he thought it still possible she may come back to him. Even if after reading the card, not nearly as much as he once had.

Part Two: The Fishing Tournament

When he awoke in the morning the rain the night had blown out to sea and the memories gone with it. Emmitt could see remnants—gray and threatening—on the horizon when he looked out the window. In town, though, the sky was blue and cloudless, and the air smelled clean, with just a trace of salt.

His plan for the day was to get his fishing gear organized and lay in supplies. In the past he had committed to the entire month-long Derby. The fishing tournament had been started in the late '40's by the local community as a means to raise money for their children's college education. More successful than Huff and the other founders of the Derby had imagined, the prizes for the top anglers now included a new boat, along with various cash awards and fishing gear for the runners-up. Hunkered down over the oak table after a long day of fishing, Huff and he would talk late into the evenings, tide tables and charts spread out before them, drinks at their elbows, usually one of Huff's Camels smoldering in the ash tray, the two anglers planning their strategy for the next day's fishing. Dana enjoyed watching the two men at their labor of love. It was reassuring to know he could look up and catch her eye— to see her smiling at him from across the room.

Of course, this year it was all different. He'd given himself two weeks to see how things went. Just in case the memories were too much. Just in case he had to flee.

Grocery-wise, he figured it best to buy for one week at a time. But there were things to do before that. After a light breakfast at the diner, he caught the bus out to the airport to pick up a rental car. On his way back to Ferry Town he stopped at Sherm's Bait & Tackle to purchase a Derby stamp; provisions at the A&P would follow that. While waiting for Harry to process the entry form, Emmitt leafed through the new Derby book. He was always amazed at how many times Huff had either won the Derby outright, or at least the flyrod category. His old pal's name was listed there for the first time in 1948. That was the year Emmitt had been born. A lot had happened in the intervening fifty-odd years, all of it leading up to a simple moment when Huff's name, listed in the Past Winners section, would never be listed as a recent winner again.

Maybe this is my year, he thought, as Sherm handed him his Derby pin across the counter and showed him where he could pick out his choice of Official Derby ball caps. Biggest striper, maybe? Or a false albacore, "albie" for short? He didn't fish for the bluefish, though if he happened to catch one big enough to weigh in he certainly would.

Not that winning had ever been his reason for the fishing. Being a part of it was good enough especially the time spent with Huff on the water and with Dana on the island. Knowing the entry fee went to college scholarships for the island kids had been good, too. Huff craved the competition, always advising him to not divulge to *anyone* where they caught fish or thought fish might be. Huff also relished the remembrance of his victories in the cold months when no fishing was to be had. Every man needed something to get him through the winter Huff told him. His memories of the fall fishing were Huff's. For Emmitt, Dana and his writing had been enough. Now only one would have to suffice.

As he left the store, Derby cap on and carrying a plastic bag containing leaders, tippet, and flies, Emmitt saw two fishermen walking up from the parking lot. Still in their waders, one of them held a snapped-off rod in his hands. And that was how the Derby went, Emmitt thought when he was back in the rental car. Hard fishing. And sometimes hard luck. And the dream of a payoff of some kind when it was all over. Suddenly, he was excited to get to it.

After putting away the groceries he'd purchased at the A&P, Emmitt took a mug of hot coffee and walked down Dock Street to Soldier's Wharf. From the top of the covered wharf he had a great view of the harbor, the south end of the island where it looped back around on itself forming a big lagoon, the famous Cut. Without binoculars he couldn't see them, but he was sure they were there: fishermen lining both banks of the Cut, flyrods or spinners in hand as they waited on fish and false albacore, coming in or out of the narrow passage on the tide. He would join them tomorrow. Either there, or up at Quohog Beach. It would depend on the tides and how he felt in the morning when the alarm went off.

There were boats moving out through the harbor, cruising slowly in the no-wake zone until they reached the point and the lighthouse. He had some ideas of where they might be headed, but the fish changed from day to day, and you could never be sure. When fishing the Derby you had to stay alert to the changes in weather, the tides, what the wind did, where the birds went, what bait fish the predators were feeding on, and where that bait fish was located on any given day. A brand new fully rigged twenty foot Boston Whaler was a nice prize—it behooved a man to pay attention.

Emmitt's fishing would all be from shore, though, now that Huff was gone. He'd still have to be aware of the conditions, but his range of search was narrowed some. Rory had inherited his father's boat, the old and well-used open fisherman, and Emmitt was sure if he asked Rory would take him offshore. But Rory was busy, between his family, the bike shop, and his fledgling construction business, and didn't really have the time. Besides, Emmitt didn't like asking. There were plenty of fish to be caught from shore. It was simply up to him to do so.

***

Using Dana's old recipe, that night he made beef stew. The act of cooking—cutting the meat into small cubes, slicing the carrots, potatoes, and onions, combining all the ingredients together, and stirring the simmering mass in the big cast iron pot—kept Emmitt from his thoughts. While the stew bubbled away on the stove he sat at the table with the tide chart and a glass of red wine, ostensibly in honor of his dead wife and her stew he was preparing.

According to the chart, if he wished to fish at daybreak with an incoming tide the Cut was out. The tide wouldn't be right there until almost noon. Quohog Beach looked to be his best bet. And that was perfectly fine with him. He'd wake while it was still dark, pack a lunch and a thermos of coffee along with his tackle bag and rod, and drive his rental car up to Quahog. It was a half mile walk down the beach to the Bowl and the first little point jutting out into the sound. He would begin his fishing there. Sitting at the oak table, the last of the day's light vanishing over the harbor and the small room enveloped by the odor of the cooking stew, he thought of daybreak at Quohog. He tried very hard not to think of Dana and how she wasn't there with him.

The stew wasn't quite right. He must have goofed on the amount of spices, too much, or too little, he wasn't really sure. It tasted flat, not at all like his wife's had tasted, not as he remembered at any rate, and he drank more of the red wine than he planned. He dozed off in the recliner after eating, the little TV in the room tuned to a network show he didn't pay any attention to. When he jerked awake the eleven o'clock newscast was almost over, and he had spilled his last glass of wine on the hardwood floor. He found some paper towels under the sink and after cleaning up the mess stumbled into the berth and was immediately asleep.

He had dreams of Dana, moving from one fogged image to another. She came to him first in these dreams, at the bookstore her father owned on Boylston Street in Boston. Then the dream changed, and they were alone in the room above the bike shop. It was the day Dana had caught her first albie on a flyrod. She'd battled the fish all up and down the beach, her hair a mass of bouncing curls flying in the wind as she ran on the shoreline, doing her best to keep the rod tip up, doing her best to keep pressure on the fish as both Emmitt and Huff, running behind her, were urging her to do.

That had been a good day. In the small room that night she had turned in his arms. Her eyes glowed in the candlelight as she said, "I see now why you love catching them so." Dana kissed him, her lips tasting faintly of wine. "But don't ever love them more than you love me."

He'd assured her it was not possible—that he could never love anything more than her.

Now, in his pleasant state of dreaming, he waited for her to turn to him again and speak, repeat those words from before. But when she did it was her sick face that he saw, wrinkled and shrunken, her eyes dull with the morphine and pain. He didn't want to, but he drew back. Dana smiled, that wan little forced grin she'd managed all those last days of illness.

"You should have done more, Emmitt," she said in the dream. "I loved you. It seems you could have done more."

When the alarm went off at five he was already awake, and staring out the window at the blackness.

***

The jetties lining both sides of the inlet into Quohog Harbor were already crowded with anglers when Emmitt arrived. It had been dark as he made the twenty-mile drive from Ferry Town, the headlights cutting along the two lane road occasionally picking up the running forms of startled deer, creatures like him just beginning to stir in the early hour. Now the sun was barely up, a small edge of red orb rising in the east behind him as he walked the path along the dunes down to the beach. He was not surprised to see all the fishermen on the rocks, and in fact, had expected it. Some of them, he was sure, had been there all night, fishing for the big stripers that came into the harbor to feed. Others were like him, there early to catch the morning albacore run. The number of men fishing, though, was a good sign. Albies had been caught there in recent days. If they hadn't the jetties would be empty, save for tourists, or newcomers to the fishing scene of Squanocket.

The path dead ended on the beach. Instead of walking up on the rocks he continued south on the sand, toward the bowl, a half of mile in the distance and a spot good to him in the past. Two men were down that way, their dark shapes against the sand in the pale light. With the tide at dead low, his wading boots crunched on the shells left behind in the wet sand by the receding water. Gulls wheeled and dipped some fifty yards off shore, their sharp cries ringing out in the otherwise quiet morning. The ocean was calm in the shelter of the sand and dunes, but the wind coming out of the northeast was building, ruffling the water further out. Albies liked to feed in a light chop such as that, and Emmitt knew those crying gulls were anxious, waiting like the humans for the fish to show.

An old washed-up log lay half-buried in the sand above the high water mark, just before the belly of the bowl. He stashed his tackle bag and thermos by the log and walked down to the water. The day was coming up clean and cool with the sun, the only clouds in the sky being a few thin strips of white far off to the west. Along with the sun the wind rose faster, pushing the water against the shore in small waves that crashed over the tops of Emmitt's wading boots. As he unlimbered his fly rod, it was beginning to happen. True, it was nothing visible that he could see. But he could certainly feel the tension racing along the beach as anglers, those on the jetties, and those on the shore, looked out over the water.

Then, on some unseen, unheard, signal of their own, the birds working off shore moved in. After making a cast in the general direction of the gulls, Emmitt looked down in the water just past the shore break. A thick line of bait fish swam slowly against the incoming tide. Soon the albies would move in on them and the bite would be on.

As if to prove this true, a loud, "Ya-haa," came from down the beach. Turning toward the sound he saw one of the two anglers braced against a fish, the man's rod bent at a ninety degree angle, fly line glistening in the morning light as it sailed out above the water. The other angler gestured wildly at his partner's rapidly disappearing line, waving his hands and yelling as the albie made his first initial run.

It wasn't such a good thing to do. Alerting others to incoming fish. Emmitt suddenly thought of Huff. Could see his old fishing partner shaking his head in amazement at such antics. Could almost hear him saying how that's no way to win a tournament.

Then they were there, right in front of him: the rest of the school of false albacore, slashing their way through the line of bait fish in the surf. He froze for a moment, watching the wild upward spray from the feeding fish as they churned the water—then made a long cast in front of the oncoming albies. The cast was a good one, the white and yellow fly dropping ten yards in front of what he hoped was the lead fish. Emmitt stripped the fly line hand over hand into the stripping basket at his waist. Nothing happened and he lifted the line and recast, and he too, had a fish on, the reel screaming as the albie, in what seemed hardly more than a blink of an eye, raced for the wide open sea.

With that first surging run of the hooked albacore it was like he had never been gone from the island and that nothing had changed.

The fish came through for a while that morning, mostly small schoolies. They were fun to catch, but with none weighing more than five or six pounds, too small to take back to Ferry Town to weigh in at Derby headquarters. Emmitt enjoyed the action while it lasted, though, hooking up on four fish, three of which he landed. The one that broke him off felt bigger than the others. When he was reeling in the slack fly line and leader, he thought that fish *might* have been worth weighing. Hell, if not for the Grand Prize, then perhaps for a weekly. Get his name on the leader board. For a little while, maybe.

He caught himself at this and laughed as he waded back down to the surf after tying on fresh tippet and a new fly. That was Huff talking. Not him. He wasn't there to win anything.

When the tide lulled around mid-morning, Emmitt took a break from standing in the surf and blind casting while waiting for the albies to come back. They did this: vanished sometimes in the middle of the tide, only to return at the top of it for a last slashing go-round before the tide came full. He walked back up to the log where he'd stashed his tackle bag and thermos and sat on the aged piece of driftwood. The log had been on the beach a long time, almost as long as he'd been fishing there and that was close to twenty years. It was a good place to sit and enjoy a cup of hot coffee. A good place to regroup and wait for the next round, so to speak.

Something caught his attention, some sort of movement in the corner of his right eye. Turning, Emmitt saw, striding along the sand toward him, a tall, blond man. Well over six feet, the man wore camouflage chest waders, with a fly rod slung cavalier-like over his right shoulder. Long straw colored hair flowed down his shoulders and back. Behind him by a step or two came a woman, shorter than the man by a foot. She, too, was dressed in camo-patterned waders and carrying a fly rod. Bringing up the rear were two men in jeans and turtleneck sweatshirts. They looked odd enough with how they were dressed, which obviously was not for the fishing. Even odder were the canvas gear bags these two men lugged over their backs as they struggled to keep up. The canvas bags, as Emmitt soon discovered, were filled with cameras, camcorders, and sound equipment.

As he passed by in front of Emmitt the tall blond acknowledged him with a curt nod. The blond man had the ruddy features of someone from the Dutch, or German regions of Europe. The woman—who acknowledged Emmitt with a tight smile, instead of a quick nod—looked more along Mediterranean lines. Her dark hair, cut short, framed her olive skin, visible beneath the wide brim fisherman's hat she wore. She was a good looking woman Emmitt decided in the brief moment he had to observe her. Well built. One would have to be blind not to notice the black eyes she flashed at him as she walked by.

"Ja. This is good."

Judging by guttural tones of the man's voice Emmitt's assumption of the man's origins seemed to be on the money. Who or where he was from was actually immaterial. It was only Emmitt's writer's curiosity that always had him trying to place people. More to the point was the fact of the man's rudeness. How, instead of moving on down the beach to allow plenty of space between him and Emmitt, and the two anglers even further down, he stopped hardly ten yards away from where Emmitt had set up camp.

"Ja," he barked out to the others coming up. "We start here."

The new-comer's behavior was rude, beyond the pale. Moving in like that on another's spot went against all fishing courtesy, un-written as it might be. If Emmitt were rude like these people he might have said something. Had Huff been there he would have. Would let them know in no un-certain terms what he thought about their rudeness.

But Huff wasn't there. Too surprised to say anything, Emmitt watched as the man and the woman walked down to the surf, stripping line off their reels as they went. The other two men busied themselves setting up the cameras and sound equipment. At a sign from the man holding the camcorder, the blond began a monologue in German, casting, and talking, sometimes turning to smile at the camera, the white teeth in his ruddy face flashing in the mid-morning sunlight. A flock of gulls came wheeling overhead and he pointed at them, making an aside to the woman fishing in the surf next to him as he did so. Following the flight of the gulls, Emmitt saw a school of albies down the beach, slashing at baitfish. The man saw them too, pointing his rod tip at the approaching fish and speaking rapidly to the camera.

Then the fish were there. The man made a long, effortless, cast and he was on, the rod bowed with the pressure of the fish, the reel screaming as the albie took line. A second later the woman let out a grunt and set up on another one. The two fought the fish for a while, standing apart from one another in the surf, rods bent toward the fish racing out into the sound. Gulls wheeled over the remnants of the baitfish the albies had decimated, while Emmitt, up on the log, watched the fishing scene unfold before him. At one point, the man turned to the camera man behind him on the beach, holding his rod up in one hand. The long graphite tube bent sharply over the water, the tip vibrating with the pressure of the fish.

"Ja! Ja!" The blond pointed at the camera with his free hand. "You see? This is easy. Ja?"

It took him a second before Emmitt realized the blond was addressing him. The camera man turned to him up on the log, the sun light glinting off the glass lens of the camcorder. Just like that it was his fifteen minutes of fame. Not knowing what else to do Emmitt waved and tipped his hat to the man in the water. Local color, he thought, as the camera man went back to filming the German and his fish. That's all he was to them. A nice, homey touch to the film they were making.

The man and woman landed their fish about the same time, walking the tired albacore out of the water, backwards up on the beach where the fish lay flopping on the sand, the powerful tails of the spent fish still fighting, trying to gain some sort of purchase in the loose sand of the beach. The albies were the same size as the others that had been coming through that morning. It was funny, but Emmitt was glad for that. If the two intruders who blundered purposely into his spot had caught, right off the bat, big, respectable fish, it would have added salt to the wound.

After releasing their catch the man and woman turned to the camera and smiled, before wrapping each other in a tight embrace long and lovingly on the beach. Emmitt ached watching the couple. He had made love with Dana once, up in the dunes behind the log. It was after a day very much like the present one, when both of them had caught nice fish and lost some as well. She'd wrapped game hens in a picnic basket along with a bottle of Merlot. When they broke for lunch after fishing hard all morning, the cold hen and lukewarm Merlot had tasted very good. He knew they had brought a blanket along—was hoping for a chance to use it.

After eating the slightly decadent lunch, and seeing that the beach was practically deserted, it seemed the chance was at hand. But when he reached out to pull her down with him Dana resisted.

"Not yet, you horny man!" She ran off laughing down the beach when he persisted, her brown curly hair bouncing in the sun, yelling out over her shoulder, "There's fish still to be caught. The other can wait!"

God yes, and hadn't the wait that day been worth it, Emmitt thought, remembering how as the sun was going down over the beach they had wrapped themselves up in the blanket and made slow love until the sun was completely gone.

The German couple broke off their embrace, and while the film crew reloaded the man and woman went back to the work of fishing. They made a good team, he decided. Respected each other's cast. Helped whichever one was on to land the fish. Identical waders were a little much, perhaps, but probably good for the filming. Besides, who was he to say? Hell, if he'd thought Dana would go along with it, he might have got them identical waders.

With that image he decided he'd had enough. He had been okay until the man and woman anglers kissed, and Dana came flooding in again. Though the memory was a good one, these days pain came always on the heels of such memories. The beach was too crowded now, anyway, what with the film crew and some other fishermen that had come straggling down. The fishing had been good. He might come back tomorrow. Or maybe hit the Cut. It didn't matter. He was done for today. Picking up his tackle bag and thermos he started up the beach toward the jetties.

"You're leaving?" The woman turned and gave him a shy smile as he walked past her.

"Good luck," he told her, surprised to hear an American accent. "It's all yours now."

"Don't let us run you away. There's plenty of room for all of us."

He waved and continued walking. He meant it, about the luck. He turned to look back once, when he was almost to the jetties, and saw how they'd wasted no time in replacing him with their canvas bags of gear on the log. But the woman was wrong about there being plenty of room. When he started remembering his wife, how it all used to be, there was room for nothing else.

***

That night he walked down to the Bramford House on North Bay Street for dinner. The Bramford, an old Victorian structure three stories high, had been home to a whaling captain and his family in the days when whaling drove the economy of the area. His descendants still lived on the property and ran the restaurant and hotel they had converted the home into back in the 50's. A large oil painting of Captain Bramford hung above the brick fireplace in the main dining room, a stern looking man with one hand tucked Napoleon-like in his captain's jacket as his hard eyes stared out over his domain.

Despite Captain Bramford the dining room was very cozy, warmed by the blaze in the fireplace, while oil lamps in the corners of the room cast shadows on the wood and brick walls. Paintings of Squanocket Island in the olden days graced the walls of the room, pictures of former ships that had comprised the island's famed whaling fleet and the other captains who commanded them. The food was good, simple fare, the house specialty a shepherd's pie, as well as plenty of the local seafood and thick cuts of beef.

The upper two stories contained guest rooms, and the first two years Emmitt and Dana came to the island they had stayed there. Now that the island had become an *in* resort for the movers and shakers of Manhattan, it was more money than Emmitt was willing to spend. Not that it mattered, since toward the end of their stay that second year he met Huff on the beach by Ferry Town Light, the room above the bike shop became available, and everything changed. But he always felt comfortable eating at the Bramford, in the dimly lit room with the vestiges of the past all around him, and he looked forward to his meal that night.

He was surprised to see the tall German and his lady from the beach sitting at a table by the fireplace—even more surprised when the dark woman spoke to him.

"Excuse me," she said as Emmitt passed by, following the hostess to his table. "You're the man we chased from his spot this morning." The tall blond looked up from his food when the woman spoke, giving Emmitt a dull stare before gracing him again with that curt nod of acknowledgment.

"You hardly chased me off," Emmitt told the woman. "I was done for the day."

"Perhaps. But let us make it up to you. Allow my husband and me to buy you dinner? We don't really know anyone here on the island. Other than Curt and Jurgen, who came to Ferry Town with us. So they don't count." The woman laughed as she waved her cocktail glass at the table. "Please. I mean it. Join us."

Even more surprising to Emmitt was that he accepted the invitation. Perhaps some company would be good for him, he thought. He'd done precious little interacting with his fellow human beings lately. Ever since the funeral. His talk with Rory his first day on the island had been the longest conversation he'd had with anyone in quite a while. Perhaps it's time, he told himself.

Though the food was good, a surf & turf special consisting of Maine lobster tail and a hefty cut of thick sirloin, the meal was uncomfortable. Both Dieter, as the German's name turned out to be, and his wife Elena, seemed on edge, generous invitation to Emmitt to join them beside the point. They were drinking vodka with their meal, a lot of it, and in Elena's case she appeared to be more interested in the vodka than the food. Something was on between them, and Emmitt wasn't sure if he cared to find out just exactly what that might be. It wasn't long before he regretted taking the woman up on her offer.

"We're on the island filming a documentary for 'Fly Rod Adventures.' Are you familiar with that magazine?" Elena asked Emmitt when his food came.

She had given up completely on the pretense of eating, and having set her dinner off to the side, sipped steadily from her cocktail. The fingers of the hand holding the glass—long and elegant, the nails carefully taken care of—seemed to Emmitt better suited for the world of flashy hotels and five star restaurants as opposed to a rustic inn on a semi-remote New England island casting a fly rod on a windy beach. Yet she had handled herself well that morning with the rod.

"I'm afraid I'm not," Emmitt answered. He washed down a bite of lobster with the Merlot. Both lobster and the wine were very good. Even if he had the feeling they would both taste better if he were anywhere other than where he was. "But it certainly sounds like pleasant work."

"It can be."

Her eyes narrowed some as she put her drink down and looked at him across the table. She was taking his measure, Emmitt saw. Trying to figure out if he were genuinely interested, or just being polite.

"Doing that kind of work must take you to some pretty fabulous places," he said, in hopes of reassuring her.

"Ja." Dieter tossed down the last of his vodka and wiped the corners of his mouth with the cloth napkin. His plate was picked clean, his face, already ruddy, even redder from the alcohol. "We fish good all over."

"Some of us fish good," Elena said and smiled, a very pleasant one Emmitt thought. "Dieter didn't do as well as he would have liked."

The German jerked his head around to glare at her before signaling to the waitress to bring more drinks.

Elena laughed. "My husband, Mr. Raines, is still enveloped in the old macho European mind set. He doesn't like it when I out-fish him. A rarity, for sure," and she smiled again.

"Lucky," Dieter grunted as he looked around impatiently.

"That mindset is not limited to European males," Emmitt said. "I can assure you of that. My wife liked to fish, though not as much as I. She would have been very good at it if she'd put as much energy into as I used to. But out fishing me? That could be tough to take, I imagine."

"Ah." Along with Dieter's the waitress had brought her a fresh drink, and Elena held the glass lovingly in her hand for a second before taking a long gulp. "You were alone on the beach this morning. And now. Your wife's not in the mood to join you?"

"My wife's dead."

It never felt right saying such a thing, especially now when the only reason he did so was for some sort of petty shock value.

"I'm sorry to hear that," the woman said after a bit. "Really sorry."

She seemed embarrassed—that embarrassment people felt when hearing something they didn't expect to hear—and for that Emmitt was sorry. Recovering herself she put her napkin on the table and said, "Excuse me, will you? I need to visit the ladies' room."

She got up unsteadily from the table and headed off across the room. As she stood up Emmitt saw for the first time how she was considerably younger than her husband. Perhaps in her mid-thirties, maybe a little older, he couldn't tell. Dieter had a good twenty years on her though.

He was also able to see what the chest waders she wore that morning did not reveal. She had firm, full breasts that strained against the black turtleneck she wore. Her legs and thighs were strong, but not overly muscular, and the black Capri pants she wore with the turtleneck displayed them well as she strode in that purposeful way of hers past the other diners crowded together in the room. Her walk was the only unwomanly thing about her. A swaying, seductive stroll would be no advantage on a windy beach or a rocking boat, where she and Dieter plied their trade for the cameras. She had it all, though: legs, hips, breasts, and buttocks, rippling beneath the clothes, all perfectly suited to her Mediterranean features. According to her, "I'm just a wholesome Italian girl, totally Americanized, born and raised in Palo Alto, CA. How I hooked up with this foreign hunk is one of the mysteries of the 20th century."

That's how she'd put it earlier when he asked about her origins. But mystery or not, she was a beautiful woman. There was no denying that.

"You like my wife?" Dieter was staring at Emmitt, who realized that he *was* staring at Elena. A slight grin split the German's lips.

"I don't know your wife."

"Ja. Me either."

Emmitt had watched the couple kissing on the beach that morning. He'd thought if their love was as good as his and Dana's they'd be okay. After spending hardly an hour with them at the dinner table he began to think the kiss he'd witnessed had been purely for the camera's sake. Elena and Dieter were nothing like he and Dana. Of that, he was certain.

"Tell me more about this work you do for the magazine," Emmitt asked when Elena finally returned from the ladies' room. Her face was freshly washed, and some eye liner reapplied, but she was unsteady on her feet as she sat back down at the table. "I've done some writing work in my time. We'll talk shop."

"Shop?" Dieter grunted into his drink.

"It's an American expression, Dieter."

The dinner crowd had thinned out, replaced by a younger, more boisterous set. Watching the National League playoff game on a TV perched on the wall behind the bar, they were talking loud, smoking cigarettes, and drinking pitchers of beer. Emmitt would have been back in his room by now—in fact thought he should go. Now, before things got out of hand at the table. Something was going on with his dinner companions. A tension he didn't know the source of, but there.

That being the case it was also true that there was nothing for him in the room. Except for the charts and tide tables. He already knew what they had to tell him about the following day and where he planned to fish. The longer he stayed at the Bramford House drinking and talking with his new acquaintances, the longer it would be before he slept. Then again, being with them a little longer just might be for the best, he decided since it may put off another night of recriminating dreams of Dana.

"Dieter and I have been with 'Fly Rod Adventures' for quite a while," Elena said, after an uncomfortable silence Emmitt was sure they all felt. "An editor there read a piece we did for 'Field & Stream' a few years back about fishing for rainbows in the mountains above Denver."

The genuine enthusiasm in her voice added to Emmitt's hope that the evening might turn out all right after all.

"He liked the photos Dieter took and the article I wrote and offered us a chance to expand our horizons. It was a good offer and paid more than Field & Stream and the other freelance work we did. Only one of us has been expanding our horizons, though."

She seemed to have really been trying to turn it around, Emmitt thought, so her last remark took him by surprise.

Dieter grunted in his drink again but said nothing. In fact, he appeared bored with the conversation, covering as it did familiar ground. But the set of his shoulders, the way his eyes strayed warily toward his wife, led Emmitt to believe the German might not be so much bored as on guard.

"The videos were my idea. We did the first one down in Costa Rica. We were on the Pacific side, going for the big sailfish there. Along with the still shots and the article, I had brought along a small camcorder. Dieter and I took turns filming. When the issue came out there was an ad at the end of the article for people wishing to buy the video. The response was good enough to encourage the editors to have us do another one. The rest as they say, is history."

"Good history, I trust," Emmitt said.

"Good fishing," Dieter said again.

"There have been some other things my husband found to be good, as well. He just doesn't like to talk about them. Do you, Dieter?"

She waited a moment for her husband to answer—laughed nervously when he did not and took another sip of her drink.

"We usually film these things in warmer climates. Florida, South America, the Bahamas. Places where I can wear a bikini, or a thong and we can get a lot of beefcake shots for the horny males in our market. Another one of my brilliant ideas, I might add. Isn't that right, Dieter?"

"Ja. Always *your* brilliant ideas."

"Oh, you've had a few in your time. But what about you, Emmitt? You said we could talk shop. What do you write?"

"Short stories. Some longer fiction. I've been able to make a living from it."

"A good living?"

She leaned across the table to Emmitt and he could see the swells of her breasts inside the turtleneck. He looked up into her eyes and she smiled, clearly aware of where he'd been looking.

"It's had its ups and downs. They made a couple of movies out of some early work I did. That paid well."

"How about sex? Is there a lot of it in your books?" She straightened up and stretched her back, pushing her breasts out. "That seems to be about as close to sex I get these days. Reading about it. Why is that, Dieter?"

She had given up completely now, Emmitt saw, and was letting the alcohol, and whatever it was between them, take her where she had decided she wanted to go.

"Shut up, Elena." Dieter stood up from the table and spying their waitress across the room he waved to her. "You've had enough." But it was clear that though the cameramen might follow his orders when he barked them out, she was a different matter.

"You see, Emmitt? Dieter gets uncomfortable when the topic comes around to sex. I've told him it's okay if he doesn't want to fuck me anymore. If he'd rather fuck those little creatures he seems to find wherever we go. Just don't get mad at me if I find someone I want to fuck. Shouldn't that be okay, Emmitt?"

"I wouldn't know."

"Maybe Dieter," Elena said suddenly to her husband, and as if Emmitt wasn't even there, "Emmitt might like to fuck me?"

And there it was. Sensing what came next, Emmitt had pushed away from the table and was about to make his goodbyes. But it was too late. Dropping the half full glass of vodka he held in one hand, Dieter snatched the dinner table up on its side. Elena had seen this coming—hell, she'd been steadily working on it for the last hour, Emmitt thought—but didn't get out of way in time. The edge of the table caught her arm with a glancing blow and sent her reeling backwards.

"Goddamn you, Dieter!"

But it was all for show. Dieter's sudden rage that really wasn't so sudden. The slight smile on her face as she glared at her husband. They had been here before. It was their scene.

Out on North Bay Street, in the darkness and quiet of Ferry Town Emmitt sucked in the clean night air. The town, except for a few restaurants open to midnight, had gone to bed. Such a waste, he thought. It should have been funny, the scene with his companions at the dining table. But it wasn't. Not even a tragedy. Just a waste.

That night he did not dream of his wife. Instead he dreamed of Elena. Of her naked breasts filling his hands as she looked into his eyes and said, "Maybe Emmitt would like to fuck me."

In the morning he felt slightly sick from all the Merlot and the anger of the night before, he thought. From being with people he didn't like. People who were rude and didn't care. Who had it all and didn't care. Unlike him, who'd had everything he wanted. Once. And who now, more than anything, wanted to have it back.

***

Three days before he was to leave Squanocket, Emmitt fished the Cut with Rory. Despite his encounter—both on the beach and at dinner with Dieter and Elena— Emmitt enjoyed his time on the island. He didn't go back to Quahog Beach or the Bramford House and that was okay. There was more than one beach on the island where he could fish and restaurants to go to when he didn't feel like cooking. Other than occasionally at evening weigh-in at the Derby headquarters, he did not see the couple again.

Because he was catching fish and the weather was good, Emmitt extended his trip from the two weeks he had originally planned on. The day after the Derby ended he would fly home and face whatever awaited him there.

Now the derby was winding down. The fish appeared to have left the waters of Squanocket Sound to head south as they always did that time of year. The islanders who'd put their work aside for the Derby were back at it, doing the best they could to earn money before winter settled fully in. It had turned cold the last few days and the late season tourists were gone as well, the beaches, and the sound, devoid of sun bathers, fishermen, and boats. Dieter was in first place on the leader board with a 12.50 pound albie, Elena was in second with a slightly smaller fish, and third place was held by a local kid who worked at Sherm's Bait & Tackle. The common consensus on Squanocket was that the Derby was over. With the fish gone the lucky anglers on the leader board appeared to have wrapped it up.

Emmitt agreed—so much so that when Rory stopped in to see him one afternoon that last week of the month, he was packing up his fishing gear for the return flight.

"Don't put it all away just yet, Mr. Emmitt," Rory said.

"No?" The boy looked so much like his father with that red hair and freckles, that eager grin. All Huff. As if his father had never left. "Now why is that, Rory? And when are you going to call me just plain Emmitt?"

"That's an awful lot of questions, Mr. Emmitt," Rory said as he came into the room. "But I suppose never."

The two men, the old and the young, chuckled together in the small room, and for a moment it was like old times, Emmitt and Huff giggling over some little joke that only made sense to them.

"Thought I would share something interesting with you. Something I just heard." When Rory spoke the moment vanished and Emmitt was back in the present. "Something good about the Cut."

"Yeah? Well then, Ror, I'm all ears."

Rory had it from a good friend—who heard it from a good friend of *his*—that albies were showing at daybreak at the Cut. Not only that, but more than just one school, feeding aggressively for an hour or so after the sun came up. There were some big fish in those schools, much bigger than Dieter's twelve pounder. The beauty of it all, according to Rory's friend's friend, was with the Derby being basically over, with people having given up, no one was fishing these albies. They were there for the taking. At least, that's what Rory had been told.

"That *is* interesting," Emmitt said when Rory was done. "Very interesting."

"I thought so." Rory grinned, his face showing his delight at sharing this good news. "What d'ya think we should do about it, Mr. Emmitt?"

"What your dad would do."

After dinner that night he sat with a brandy by the open window in the loft looking out over the harbor. He would miss this place, he thought. Like he always did when he left and it was over. Thinking of Rory and the fishing they would do in the morning it was only natural, he supposed, that his thoughts would turn to Huff and how it all began, this annual trip to the island in the fall.

***

After her father died in Boston, when the services were done and the loose ends tied up, Dana wanted to get away. She had always wanted to see Squanocket Island. Had shown him where it was on a map of New England and said, "It's supposed to be simply gorgeous in the fall, Em'."

He'd said, "Sure, why not?" and they had gone.

Emmitt had known nothing about the Derby Days Fishing Tournament. Nothing about fishing for the stripers, and blue fish, and false albacore that roamed the waters of Squanocket Sound in the fall. Only learned about it one morning when he and Dana strolled arm in arm out of the Bramford House down North Bay Street, and eventually over to Dock Street and the wharves. An old wooden building stood by the newer structure that was Ferry Town Yacht Club, the old building with a banner stretched above the double, barn-like doors of the entrance way. The banner proclaimed in bold, red, white and blue letters: *Derby Headquarters, 25th Annual Squanocket Island Blue Water Derby Days!* A couple of locals hung about in front of the building, old timers in waders and hip boots, one of them holding on to a big fish, the tails of which dragged along on the ground.

Emmitt had felt the hairs on the back of his neck stand up and turning around, saw the bike shop on the corner of Dock and Main Street for the first time. A lean, middle aged man, with a bushy shock of bright red hair on his head and an equally bright red beard, stood in the doorway of the shop, a grease stained mechanic's apron tied around his mid-section.

The following year Emmitt met a man on the beach out in front of the light house. Emmitt was struggling with a fly rod for the first time—a cheap outfit bought at a discount store off island and totally unsuited for the task he'd set for it—and a red-haired man came walking down the beach carrying his own rod. He looked again and recognized the man as the person he'd seen the year before standing in the doorway of the bike shop.

As the stranger came abreast of Emmitt he stopped to watch him cast. Fly line lay draped across Emmitt's shoulder, another wad of it in a tangle in the sand at his feet, the big, bulky fly he'd bought with the rod, bobbing in the surf just inches from the shore where no fish would ever see it, much less strike it.

"It looks like you could use some assistance, young fella," the stranger said. Though Emmitt's first thought was to tell the man to fuck off, he didn't.

"Yeah, I think I do." The two men laughed together, there on the beach, and were immediately friends.

He caught his first albie that day, burning out the drag on the cheap reel in the process, and had gone back to the Bramford House at dark to tell Dana about the crusty local he met on the beach. How he was to go to Sherm's Bait & Tackle the next day and get what this fellow Huff suggested. If he did, and if he wanted to, Huff would be at Quohog Beach the morning after that, "Say, six o'clock, young fella?"

"By God yes, Dana, I'm going to be there!"

All this in one rushing of words tumbling out of his mouth, and then it was Dana's turn to laugh. She always seemed so delighted when he was excited, when he was happy about something, one of the many qualities he loved about his wife. With the cool darkness wrapped around Ferry Town outside their room at the Bramford House, Dana sat atop the big king size bed, her hazel eyes all aglow as she rocked slightly to and fro with his excitement. "I should say so you're going, Em,'" she said—then pulled him down with her on the bed and there was no more talk of fishing, or the new pal Emmitt had made that day.

So long ago. And out of all of that in his life the only thing that remained was Ferry Town, away across the sparkling, windswept sound. To his surprise, just as he'd found himself enjoying his time on the island when he didn't think he would, this memory of the past did not hurt. Did not continue on in his sleep that night, like Dana had that first night when he over-cooked the stew and was drunk and slopped his wine on the floor and woke up in a cold sweat in the early hours not knowing where he was. Instead, Emmitt slept like the proverbial baby.When Rory came back at five the next morning Emmitt was ready, waiting out in front of the bike shop. It was still very dark, the only traffic out some early morning vendors starting their rounds in Ferry Town. The morning was bitter cold, a damp forty two degrees that with the northwest wind felt even colder. As Emmitt climbed into the cab of

Rory's beat up Blazer, he could hear the wind howling across the harbor above the truck heater ticking softly under the dash. The conditions were prefect for the Cut: northwest wind, an incoming tide, the sun just coming up. If fish were around it could be very good, but it seemed doubtful to Emmitt, that late in the season.

When he settled into his seat in the truck and Rory asked if he was all set, Emmitt said yes. They drove around the back side of the lagoon, Squanocket Pond actually, until they reached the graded road leading to the official town parking lot for the Cut. There were drives scattered along the graded road, winding through pine trees just coming visible in the half light of dawn, up to homes of the various island elite. The parking lot was their concession to the humble masses of Ferry Town, as well as the only way to keep the fishing riff raff from parking in, and blocking off, their private drives. Once parked, and after donning waders and stringing up the rods, they left the Blazer and entered a path cut into the trees and underbrush at the edge of the lot. At the end of the path wooden stairs had been built into the side of the high bluff above the water—at the bottom of those stairs was the south side of the Cut.

Emmitt paused at the top and looked out over Squanocket Sound. Off to the west lay the buildings of Ferry Town, the white and gray structures nestled snugly into the hills above the harbor. At the entrance to the harbor stood the lone sentinel of Ferry Town light. To the east was the pond, the water dark and gray in the dim light of the morning and chopped up by the winds howling through the Cut. On the far side of the inlet a four wheel drive pickup was parked on the shore, its driver standing out on the point with a big spinning rod in his hands. Other than him, and a few birds wheeling low over the water, the Cut was deserted.

They fished for over an hour into daybreak with no sign of albies. It was hard work blind casting across the northwest wind. To make matters worse, the wind drove in clumps of matted sea grass that fouled their lines and flies. If there was going to be a payoff, Emmitt thought once, as he stood in the cold water clearing wet grass from his fly, they were damn well earning it.

"I don't get it, Mr. Emmitt.

Ten yards down the beach from Emmitt, Rory stood up to his knees in the wind churned water. What had been tough casting for Emmitt did not seem to bother Rory, who laid out long casts that cut through the gusting wind to land softly sixty or seventy feet out into the channel. *He's a natural. Just like his dad*, Emmitt thought. Emmitt had been a little angry sometimes fishing with Huff. At how easy the older man made it all seem. At how hard he himself had to work for every fish he caught. Over time he lost that little anger. Learned to share the joy, just as Huff did, of each fish caught, no matter by whom. Now, at one of Huff's all-time favorite fishing spots, he hoped the first fish that morning would be caught by Rory. It seemed only fitting.

"Everything's just as Cliffie said it should be," Rory continued, cupping his mouth with one hand as he yelled into the wind. "Tide's ripping in. The fish should be here, Mr. Emmitt. Doesn't make sense."

"The minute this sport starts making sense," Emmitt yelled back, "is the minute we'd better run like hell the other way."

Rory nodded his head in agreement and went back to his casting.

"I'm sick of looking at this stretch of water." Another quarter hour had passed, with still no sign of fish. Emmitt reeled in his fly line, pushed the stripping basket on his waist around his back, and set off down the shore. "I'm going on the other side of the boathouse."

"Good luck, Mr. Emmitt." Rory grinned as Emmitt trudged by him on the sand. "I'll just keep on hammerin' 'em right here," he said, his laughter lost in the wind blowing out behind him as Emmitt walked away.

By the time the eight o'clock cannon boomed in Ferry Town the tide was almost full, the last flushing run of the incoming water starting to go slack. The morning had come on full as clear and cold, the surface of the pond and the Cut a sparkling blue. Still, the fish had not shown. He continued with the blind casting, but it was hard to stay focused on fish he couldn't see.

When he looked back up the shore line, after yet another fruitless cast, he saw that Rory was out of the water, sitting down with the coffee thermos up past the high water mark. It seemed like a good idea to Emmitt. He might as well reel it in and go join the kid. The fish, whatever schools of them Rory's friend's friend had seen, were gone now. He had tried, which was all he could do. It was time to just call it a day.

But as he began cranking the fly line in, out of the corner of his eye he saw a splash off shore. Then the water at his feet erupted. Fish slamming bait all around him. Albies he could see in the clear shallows. Large fish, right there at his feet, all in the flash of an instant, coming in when he was off guard. More of them than he had seen all Derby—and he was not ready.

There was nothing he could do about it. Except what he did—a quick, half-ass roll cast, lifting the rod tip up and in, and flipping the twenty feet of fly line floating out in the slackening current, over with his right wrist. Beyond the disappearing splash of the fly hitting water was a swirl of light, a swirling flash of color, Emmitt instinctively knew was fish.

One of those big albies the friend's friend had spoken of. Bigger than the twelve pounder Dieter held first place with. Big enough to win the Derby with.

Another flash of color swirled in the water where he had cast, and Emmitt stripped the line. Sudden none of it mattered. A hard, solid yank on the other end of the line as the fish took the fly. A steady lift of the rod tip, just as Huff had taught him all those years before. And just like that, Emmitt was on fish.

And just like that, with fish stripping line off the reel in a searing run for freedom, and Rory running down the beach towards him yelling out, "Don't lose him Emmitt! For God's sake don't lose him! And for the first time in the last six months Emmitt felt alive.

Part Three: Foreign Shores

Two years later, and not sure of the right Metro stop, on the Friday afternoon of his second week in Paris, Emmitt Raines called for a cab. Fortunately, the landlady kept the numbers for two different ones posted on the refrigerator. Three months shy of his fifty-fourth birthday in December, Emmitt had a dinner date for the evening. It took a bit, what with his very little French and the dispatcher's equally limited English, but he was able to arrange for a taxi to pick him up at eight that night. He was to meet Sylvie—the landlady of the Airbnb where he was staying—at her apartment and was a little nervous as he waited for the cab. But he had called her and was going.

Then the cab was there, the driver blowing the horn, and Emmitt hurried down the narrow stairway of the apartment building and out the door.

The cabbie, of Middle East origin and indeterminate age, shook his head when Emmitt told him the address. Handing the driver the card Sylvie had given him outside of the Moulin Rouge, Emmitt pointed to the address on it. After punching the number into the portable GPS on the dashboard, the driver nodded his head and said, "Oui."

The warm, heavy air of the first part of the week was gone. Now, the evening was cool and comfortable and Emmitt rode with the window down as the cab rolled along the streets of Paris with all the lights coming on at dusk. He was to meet her at eight thirty and had plenty of time to get there. *Plenty of time to change his mind*—but the cab was pulling up at the apartment building sooner than Emmitt had expected, and suddenly there was no time left at all.

"7 Rue de Charlus." The driver, his head turned to Emmitt in the backseat, pointed to the building on the right. "Monsieur?"

"Oui." Emmitt counted out the fare and handed it to the waiting cabbie. "Merci." And then he walked into the apartment building lobby, up the circular stairs to the fourth floor where he rang the bell at Sylvie's apartment.

"Ah yes, Emmitt. Bonsoir."

She stood in the soft light of the open door, looking every bit as fantastic as she had at the Moulin Rouge and because of this, Emmitt did not know what to say.

"Did you just arrive? Or have you been pacing the hallway wondering if you should ring my bell, after all?"

So his nervousness showed. Thankfully Sylvie, with her little bit of playfulness, knew how to ease it. Much as she had the other night at the Moulin Rouge when he did not recognize her at first, mumbled an apology, and with a little wave of her hand, waved all of it away.

"No, that's not what I've been doing," Emmitt said. "I just got here a second ago. Besides, you look stunning."

"Merci, Emmitt. You're too kind."

"No, I mean it. You look fabulous."

It was true. The tight fitting pantsuit, high heels, and lips colored a deep red, were unlike anything he had seen on a woman he dated. Of course, it wasn't like he had dated lately. She'd done some things to her hair as well, so that now, instead of how it had been that night at the Moulin Rouge, it seemed a different color—he couldn't be sure. The way she had pulled it back tight from her face served to highlight very well both her face and the large, primitive sort of earrings she was wearing. All in all, the word fabulous, being the best he could come up with at the time, as far as he was concerned didn't really do her justice.

"Really?" Her smile seemed honest enough, Emmitt thought. And not some dating game she was playing—admittedly one Emmitt was not playing either and in fact had no idea how to. "You truly like?"

"Yes. I *truly* do."

"Again, thank you. But come in, please. I just returned from dropping Coralie at the sitter. You know how four-year olds can be. Especially girls. Tonight she was even fussier. So sadly, I am running a little behind. With a couple of things still to do before we go, yes?"

"Sure," he said, not that he had any experience with four year olds, male or female. And then with a little smile to hide his embarrassment, "Hopefully nothing to do with what you're wearing. I feel a little under-dressed as it is."

"No, no," she said. He was happy to see she was smiling, too. "A phone call I should have made earlier. Business and important so I need to attend to it. And you look fine, Emmitt. Perfectly fine."

Which brought some comfort—even if he still felt the grey slacks and corduroy blazer he was wearing were in-adequate, considering how she was dressed, for the occasion.

"But please, come in, come in," she said, as she had just a minute before, quickly taking him by the hand as if she realized the situation suddenly. "The neighbors will think I am some sort of rude woman. Or worse. Leaving my guest so long in the hallway."

Once inside she steered him inside to a little sofa in the living room. "I won't be long, I promise. Are you hungry?"

"A little bit." Close like that he could smell her perfume, musky and pleasantly arousing, vaguely familiar as well. "But there's no hurry. The fragrance you're wearing?"

"Yes? You like? Vanille patchouli by Molinard. My favorite."

"I like very much." He did—and the patchouli explained it, not Vanille by Molinard, but still, the same perfume Dana had favored. With that he was glad Sylvie left the room. Hopefully the phone call she had to make would give him enough time to put Dana out of his mind.

The inside of her apartment was in stark contrast to the hard dullness of the building's hallway. A rustic wooden table by the door held a glass vase with some kind of branches arrayed inside it. Beside the vase, a box of crayons and next to the crayons, a Mac laptop, closed, the power cord trailing on the floor. All the rooms, kitchen and bath included, were painted in a glossy crimson color, while low leather furniture—a sofa, some comfortable chairs—snugged up against the walls of the living room, a glass coffee table on a bright, and ethnic patterned rug in front of the leather sofa. On the wall above the sofa hung a large print, splashes of color, mixed with black and white that swirled around words that could be French, but then again, maybe not. On the wall across from the sofa, arrayed in a pyramid, was a trilogy of photographs, apparently by the same photographer, and dealing with street scenes of the Philippines where peasant children looked up at the camera with curious eyes.

The print and photographs were interesting—but what caught Emmitt's attention came from behind the closed door of Sylvie's bedroom: muffled music, strange, soft, laced with unfamiliar drumbeats and rhythms. Suddenly, Emmitt wondered what Sylvie's bedroom looked like—and with her in it.

And just as suddenly, all thoughts of Dana were gone.

There was a book on the coffee table in front of the sofa, a faded red covered hardbound. Though the title was in French, what with the author's name below—Albert Camus—Emmitt could see that it was a copy of *The Stranger* by the famous French writer. He opened the cover and on the flyleaf was a handwritten inscription, again in French, and that he didn't understand, other than Camus' signature at the end.

"We have a little time before we go," Sylvie said as she came in. She carried two wine glasses filled with a red . "One glass of wine is okay, I hope?"

"Very much so," Emmitt said as they clinked glasses together.

"I hope you like what I have done with my apartment" Sylvie said. "After the divorce, with all of Gerald's thing gone, I was able to make this place my own."

Fortunately for him, Emmitt realized, her accent—even her laughter—were just French enough to remind him that patchouli or not, beautiful woman or not, she was not Dana. Nor even close to any of the few women he had known in the past.

"I guess I have to tell you again," he said. He had briefly considered moving away a little from the contact of thigh upon thigh. But only briefly, and stayed where he was. "But 'monsiuer' isn't necessary. And yes, I do like what you have done here"

"Good! 'Monsieur' is so stuffy. My parents raised me with proper manners, I guess. In this day and age I find it useful to be stuffily polite at first. Especially with Americans. No offense, Emmitt. Still, you Americans are hard to figure out." She laughed, then noticing the book he still held in his hands, said, "You like Camus?"

"Yes, I do," he said, debating again a little if he should move away some on the sofa—quickly deciding there was no need. "I haven't read this since high school but remember it as being very powerful."

"I, too, read him in high school," she said. "Camus was a friend of my Gran Mama's. He wrote such a lovely inscription for her. Praising her for her bravery and friendship during those troubled days."

"Troubled days?"

"Oh yes, the war you know. They fought together in the Resistance." Her brown eyes were lit up with the memory, the wine glass, still half full, held forgotten in her hand. "The Nazis killed her first husband, for he was Jewish. My grandmother joined the Resistance after that, where she met Camus, served as a courier for him. She was a brave woman, indeed."

"Sounds it," Emmitt said, though he couldn't help thinking of his father who had also been in that war, and not so brave, judging by what he had done when he came home.

"Gran Mama and he stayed in touch for a long time after the war, though by then she had met my grandfather and married him. She had coffee with Camus a few weeks before he died. It was the last time she saw him. She said she could tell he was troubled by something but he would not tell her. Sad, yes?"

"Very sad, and those were troubled days indeed, both during the war and after."

"Oh yes, and still troubled now, with Al Qaida and what happened in your country, and all, wouldn't you say?" But her face lit up then in a little smile as she took another sip of wine. "But tonight is tonight, Emmitt, and no time for talk of troubles."

"Agreed," Emmitt said. He frowned, looked at the wine glass in his hand, and then said, "You know, I almost didn't call—wasn't sure your offer was a serious one."

"I'm glad you *did* call, Emmitt. My offer was indeed a serious one."

"I'm honored then," he laughed.

"Oui. You should be."

Suddenly she kissed him, lightly, but on the lips. Surprising as the kiss was to him, just as surprising was how when she went to pull away, Emmitt stopped her, put his arms around her waist, and kissed her back.

"Come," she said when she *did* pull away. "The night is young and we have reservations down the street."

"You've thought of everything," he said, glad that she had, for he certainly had not. Glad suddenly, too, that he was with her.

"Yes, I have."

This Friday night in Paris was off to a very good start, he thought, as the two of them walked down the flight of stairs and out into the street. Maybe even enough of a good start that for a few hours, at least, he could forget about why he had come to Paris in the first place.

*****

The only complaint he had about the second-floor apartment on rue Ravignan was the bar three doors down. It wasn't open during the day, but at night the noise the bar's patrons made into the early hours of the morning came loud and clear through the open windows. When the nights were cool he could close the insulated double windows of the bedroom and be comfortable. But a spell of several very warm days the second week he was there forced him to keep the windows open. It was either that or suffocate in the tiny, un-air conditioned bedroom.

The music, laughter, the conversations of the predominately youthful patrons, melodious as they were in their native French, kept Emmitt awake until closing time. As the drunken youths stumbled off along the cobblestoned street, he lay and listened to the sound of them fade away in the night. It was then that he could finally sleep. Those nights were the only time during his stay at 4 rue Ravignan, and in Paris, that he was glad Dana was not with him.

She had always wanted to go to France, to Paris in particular; had told him as much not long after they first met. It wasn't that Emmitt didn't want to. It was just that things kept coming up, especially after his second book came out with good reviews. There was the book tour, the interviews on TV and the radio. When that settled down, they decided that in September—to celebrate both the success of the book and their second anniversary—they would go.

But right before Labor Day, out of the blue Dana's father passed away. Mr. Kincaid had owned the bookstore around the corner from the Parker House in Boston where Emmitt first met Dana. Because of this, as well as the fact that Mr. Kincaid had welcomed Emmitt without reservation into his daughter's life, Emmitt was just as surprised and saddened as his wife over this loss.

Instead of exploring Paris at their leisure, they wound up spending most of that September settling Mr. Kincaid's affairs in Boston. Once that was done, on a whim and because it was close by, they went to Squanocket Island. France was put on the back burner.

They had been married five years when Dana discovered she was pregnant—a discovery she shared with him over dinner one March evening. It had been raining all day, one of those northeasterly storms common that time of year, which the hot days of summer would put an end to. Through the open windows Emmitt could hear the last of the storm dripping from the leaves of the palm trees as he sat down at the table. On the other end of the table Dana was setting out dinner, fried chicken from a stand up on Federal Highway that always came fresh and with all the good Southern trimmings. It was a meal they allowed themselves to enjoy every once in a while, usually on minor special occasions. Tonight, though, Emmitt couldn't think what that special occasion might be. He didn't have long to wait before he found out.

"I went to the doctor today," Dana said as she tucked a napkin into her lap.

"Really?" He looked up, curious because she hadn't mentioned she was going, and a little worried, too. "Is everything okay?"

"Better than okay. The rabbit died."

"Excuse me?"

"I'm pregnant, you goof!"

Emmitt didn't know what to say. A pregnancy, a baby, was not something he had put a lot of thought into. He had always supposed it might occur some day, but with that, always hoped that that day was a long ways off. But he knew enough right then to get up from the table and take her up in his arms.

"That's good news, then," he told her.

"Yes," she said, against his neck. He could feel her tears on the skin above his shirt collar. "It's very good news. Thank you, Emmitt. Thank you very much."

Only, over the next few days Emmitt began to wonder if it really was good news. He would have liked someone other than his wife to talk to about it. His mother was dead—father, too—and there was no one close at hand *to* talk with. Huff on Squanocket and Howard Kamen, his agent in New York, were the only men he considered friends. Emmitt's doubts about parenthood were a subject about which Huff would not be sympathetic. Being a father of five, Huff obviously had no fears. Howard was a father as well, but he had listened to Emmitt in the past when he had worries other about things, mainly whether or not he was really a good writer. Howard had stood as best man at his wedding, had even thrown a bachelor party of sorts for him, even if it consisted of only the two of them getting very drunk at a strip club in Miami. Howard would have to do.

"I think you're making a big deal about nothing, my man," Howard told him over the phone. "Men become fathers every day and seem to get on with their lives just fine."

"Jesus, Howard, but I'm uncomfortable with this."

"You mean scared?"

"Yeah." And he was, too. "I don't know the next thing about being a father. Or babies, for that matter."

"No one does until it happens. Trust me, I know."

Emmitt knew that to be the case. There were three Kamen girls; his wife Mary Kamen being Catholic, the pill was not an option, as Howard had complained to Emmitt the night of the bachelor party.

"What about my work?" It was Emmitt's last protest. "How am I going to write with a kid crawling around?"

"Other writers, many of them much better than you, have figured out a way." There was a pause and a slight crackle on the bad connection. "At least you're not a drunk. You've got that going in your favor. Drunks are terrible fathers. And mothers for that matter. They smother their child with love or ignore them all together. The way my father did with me. Either way, the child gets screwed up."

"Well, just like babies, I don't know anything about drunk parents," Emmitt said, curious where Howard was going. "My mother liked a glass of wine and a cocktail before dinner when she was out. That was the extent of it. Hell, I like a good drink myself. As for my father, you know how I feel about him. And I have no idea if he was a drunk or not."

"Yes, I know how you feel about your father. And for the record, I don't think you're fair to him at all."

Emmitt could feel himself get testy, the way he did whenever a conversation concerned his father. "For the record, I don't care."

"It's a moot point now. Besides, we're not talking about him, or my dad either. We're talking about you. And I have a funny feeling you're going to be just fine in the dad department."

And that was the last Howard had to say on the subject, other than to congratulate Emmitt once more, and demand to be the first one to know when the blessed bundle arrived. "Save me a cigar. A good one, too. Not one of those cheap generic baby ones." Then the line clicked dead and Emmitt was alone with his thoughts.

Not long after Emmitt and Dana's announcement the couple moved into a two story house on the 9th Street Isle. It was the same street Emmitt's grandfather and his business partner Tom Ryan had chosen as a showcase for their development plans back in the land boom of the 1920's. This was according to Emmitt's mother. Of course, as his mother went on to say, that was before the Crash and both his grandfather and Mr. Ryan, like so many other businessmen in Ft. Lauderdale and Miami, went bankrupt.

Little evidence of insolvency remained on the lovely little street now. Or in the living room of the old stucco house where Dana, surrounded by packing boxes, stood in the sunlight coming through the windows as Emmitt came through the front door pushing a handcart stacked with more boxes.

"Damn it," she said, catching him by surprise, intent as he was on navigating around the boxes spread everywhere on the bare hardwood floor. "We're going to Paris and that's it."

"Okay," he said. Looking at her—standing in the clutter of the otherwise empty room, hands on her hips, wisps of curly hair escaping from the colorful headband tied around her forehead—Emmitt saw her as he always did: a force to be reckoned with when her mind was made up. "But can we finish moving in here first?"

Jesus, he thought, remembering that day before falling asleep his first night in Paris. Could she have looked more beautiful that morning?

With the glow on her freckled face, her green eyes and oh-so-curly strawberry-blonde hair he couldn't have said no to her.

"I know it's kind of out of nowhere, baby," she said later, her breath soft and warm on his face as she spoke. "But we need to go before I'm fat and ugly and too uncomfortable to enjoy the trip."

They were lying in bed in their new bedroom listening to the night time sounds on their new street. It had begun raining that afternoon. They had been grateful, when the skies opened, that all the boxes had been unloaded from the rented truck. Tomorrow they would finish the unpacking. Tomorrow they could put the rest of their things away.

"You might get fat, but you could never be ugly."

"You're sweet. But you might rethink that when the baby's had a bad night and I come down the stairs in a ratty nightgown looking like an old crone."

He couldn't imagine such a thing, and said so.

"Just wait," she told him, giggling as she curled in closer to him. "Seriously, though, I don't want to wait until after the baby's come and he, or she, is old enough to travel. The last thing I want to do is to drag a toddler through the museums and parks and all the other glorious places and sights. Not the first time we go, at least. Call me selfish, but I'm sorry, that's just the way I feel."

He had only laughed, happy that the sickness had passed—that she was feeling good again, excited and eager to live, the way she had been before.

"I know I've always said fall was the best time to go," she went on. "But I'll be too far along by then, so we'll just have to suffer along with the tourists and the heat."

"I'm sure the suffering will be unbearable."

"That's not nice, Mister."

"What's that? Not nice?"

"Making fun of a pregnant woman," she sighed, settling back in the clean sheets. The gentle drizzle slackened off, and then stopped. Emmitt forgot about Paris, babies, all of it, as he fell off into sleep holding onto his pregnant wife. The last conscious thought he could remember was that if he wasn't happy then, he could never be.

By the middle of May they were settled into the new house and Dana went to a travel agent. That night she spread the dining room table with brochures for hotels, museums, and sightseeing trips. Together they pored over the pamphlets, finally settling on an itinerary that suited the both of them. Not wanting to waste a moment, she went back to the agent the next day. Plane tickets were purchased, a hotel reservation made, and everything was all set for them to leave on the first of July.

A week before their departure Dana woke with terrible pains. Then it was the hospital, bad news from the doctor, a miscarriage. The doctor couldn't exactly say why. Just said that they happen. No matter the why, their baby was gone.

It was all very sudden. Emmitt had thought he knew what hurting was before that morning in the hospital when the grim-faced doctor came into Dana's room. But he had been very wrong.

Well, they were both young, Emmitt just past thirty and Dana not far behind him. Life went on, everyone said. He supposed it did. Even if it seemed like not really life, but some sort of sad dream for a while. It would get better. Better enough, he hoped, that the relief he felt about the miscarriage would no longer be with him.

Because relieved was a terrible way for him to feel. No decent human being would feel that way. Yet he did. He had come to that harsh realization when she was in the hospital and he was sleeping alone in their bedroom. Just as sleep began to come, he couldn't help but think that maybe this miscarriage, sad as it was, was actually for the best. He wasn't cut out to be a father.

He had told himself for a long time that he never cared about that. That it was okay he didn't have a father. That he'd never had a chance to know the man. All he had never known about him was that he had died in the war. This turned out to be not exactly true and that Emmitt found out for himself when he was twelve. He had gone looking in his mother's bedroom one afternoon while she was at work for a book that he couldn't remember where he'd left it. The last place he tried, even though he knew it was foolish, was his mother's closet. A box on the shelf caught his eye. When he pulled it down and sat on her bed to look through it, he came upon some old photographs and newspaper clippings. One of these clippings was about a local war hero, Hilton Raines, who had died tragically in a train accident. The date of the clipping was when Emmitt's mother was pregnant with him. Not only that, but as the date revealed, the war had been over for almost two years, as Emmitt knew from his history class. Confused, he picked up the next clipping. Dated the day after the first article. This one claimed that his father's death hadn't been an accident, as first reported. No, it was a sad case of suicide.

All of this came rushing back to him as he lay alone in his and Dana's bedroom. How he had felt upon reading the second clipping and discovering that his father was no war hero at all. Audie Murphy was a hero. Sergeant York was a hero. He knew what a hero was. Read about them and saw them in the movies. His father was a coward. One who had taken his own life. Instead of taking care of his wife and the child that were coming. His son.

Emmitt's mother had come home and found him in her bedroom with the newspaper clippings. And though he had let her try to explain—how it was the war that had done that to his father. How he had come home sick with battle fatigue and malaria. That it wasn't cowardice but his illnesses that drove him to do what he did. But Emmitt didn't believe her. Though, he never told her so.

So now, a terrible thought came to him. What if he turned out to be like his father? What if he caved under the pressure of having a child— of having to give up his own life so as to take care of a boy, or girl—if and when Dana got pregnant again and he took the coward's way out? His father had. Jesus, but that idea—of killing himself—was even scarier than the others.

Full of fear and doubt and unable to sleep, he went downstairs, made a stiff drink, and sat out on the porch until dawn wondering just what kind of bastard he was.

The first time they tried to make love after the miscarriage Dana surprised him. Her face was flushed. He thought she was as eager as he was. But just as he was going to enter her, she stopped him. "I don't know if I'm ready," she told him when he rose up on his elbows to look in her eyes. "I want you, I really do," she continued. "I just don't think I'm ready. Can you understand that?"

"Yes," he said as he rolled over. Not that he was sure he really did understand. "It's okay, sweetheart. It's okay."

"Good night, Em," she said softly as she drifted off next to him. And again, "Good night."

He didn't push the issue, but was certainly happy, when over the course of the next few weeks their lovemaking became normal again—though always with protection until Dana went back on the pill.

The following year Emmitt suggested the idea of Paris. The look on her face was enough for him to know it was still too soon. They were sitting on the screened back porch, as was their habit in the early days of summer. The evenings were still cool and pleasant, not yet as humid as both the days and nights would be when July and August rolled around, smothering Ft. Lauderdale like a wet, hot blanket. Dana was drinking a glass of white Chablis and Emmitt bourbon and branch. The day had been a good one for them, what with their regular swim in the ocean off of Sunrise and A1A. When they came home the mail brought word that one of Emmitt's stories had been accepted. Not only that, but Dana's calligraphy instructor at the junior college also called to ask if she would consider being his assistant for the fall term. It didn't seem as anything could ruin the good mood they shared—but he quickly found that it could.

If the tight frown on her face were not enough, what she told him was.

"I'd be thinking of our child the whole time, Emmitt."

"But you're better now," he said.

"Am I?"

He hid in his drink, stunned at the harshness in her voice.

"Listen Emmitt," she said after a minute. "You're right. I *am* better."

"Just not that much better." He hoped there was enough lightness in his tone to put an end to how it was right then—enough to restore the good of the day they had just shared.

"Yes. Just not that much better, like you say. When I am, when I think it's right, I'll tell you."

He didn't have to ask her what "that" meant. Later, when she *was* ready, they tried hard for over a year to make a baby. When she finally did get pregnant, five months in she miscarried again. The depression and recriminations she plied on herself, despite Emmitt's objections that it was not her fault, were worse than the first time. Two years later, after a third failed pregnancy, the Raines—though it was not spoken aloud between them—gave up. Also not spoken of: France, Paris, and anything to do with those places. As he had told himself after the first miscarriage, they were young. Life went on.

***

Dana started working on her calligraphy again as the easy days of that fall rolled on, proving that life did go on. Guilt about his midnight revelation still nagged at him on occasion, especially when he came upon a father with his young son at the park or grocery store, the father proud and pleased with himself as he pushed his boy in a stroller or shopping cart. But not as often as it had—yes, life went on.

When the subject of Paris finally did come up again it was fifteen years later. Dana was very sick and unable to go anywhere. Ovarian cancer, caught too late, had her in its grip. One night near the end, even though Emmitt didn't know that at the time, in the same hospital off South Andrews Avenue in Ft. Lauderdale where he had taken her the three times before, she looked at him from the bed.

"I wish we'd gone to Paris," she said. "I really do."

"Me, too, darling," he told her, trying his best to keep a game face.

"Other than the baby," Dana continued, "It's the only thing I regret."

She looked so weak and lifeless propped up against the starched white pillows. As he had the last two days, he wondered that she was still alive.

"Our child," she suddenly said, her voice rising with some reservoir of strength he couldn't imagine. "That was out of my hands. Our hands. But Paris. We could have gone. Now I wish we had."

It was easy then for him to agree with her. About Paris at least.

She lay quiet for a while after that and Emmitt thought she had gone back to sleep—until she suddenly sat up straight.

"I think of your child, Emmitt. The little girl, Emily. Do you ever think of her?"

"Sometimes, yes. She's probably not so little anymore. She's a young woman now, I imagine."

"You, we, should have tried harder with her. At least we could have had her—sometimes—in our life. That might have helped."

A week later she was gone. Six months later—six months of grief, anger, drunkenness, and not being able to write worth a damn—on a cold and blustery New England morning at the Cut on Squanocket, the little tunys came in strong, feeding with the tide. The rush of hooking into the first really big fish of the trip had an effect on him Emmitt was not prepared for. At that exact moment—with Dana gone from his life for such a short while—Emmitt wanted to live again. Even if he wasn't sure he knew how to without her.

He had every intention of going to Squanocket again the following fall. Made that decision, in fact, while waiting for his flight at the airport on the island. He hit a wall though, once back home, one he hadn't seen coming. It concerned money, his least favorite subject.

Other than Dana's life insurance money put into some mutual funds Howard had suggested, what was left in his bank account, fueled occasionally by royalty checks from Howard, was not as much as Emmitt would have liked. The stark fact was that he would have to go back to work. Write a book, or at the very least some salable stories. The fall of 2001 and a return trip to Squanocket were a ways off yet. With a little luck he might make enough to be able to go. But as Emmitt had learned long ago, for the most part one had to make his own luck. He got to work.

The problem was the fact he was rusty. He hadn't written anything in two years, maybe longer. An idea for a book had come to him a few months before Dana became ill, a novel about his great-grandfather and his adventures fighting for the Confederacy in the Civil War, and what happened during Reconstruction in Georgia after. He had barely started on it when Dana came home from the doctor that day with the bad news. And of course, the book was put on the back burner.

He had no feeling for that project now, realized this when he took out the folder with what he had written and his notes on how the book was to proceed. Sitting at his desk one morning in October when the day was fresh and crisp outside, a cup of hot coffee at his side, he had no idea at all what he could possibly write about—what he wanted to write about. He thought suddenly of his recent time on Squanocket. Of the good fishing that last morning and Rory running down the beach at the Cut yelling at him not to lose the fish. It was a short stretch from that memory to ones of Rory's father, Huff, and the fishing and times he had shared with that man on the New England island. Two days later he had finished a memoir titled *Fishing With Huff* and mailed it off to a New England fly fishing magazine he subscribed to. Three weeks later, and much sooner than he expected, an acceptance letter arrived, along with a check. It wasn't much, both check and memoir, but it was a start.

Fueled by this, Emmitt pulled out the folder with his notes on the Civil War book, determined to bring it to life. But the folder, and all his carefully drawn up notes, looked like a foreign language to him. Worse, he didn't have any other ideas to forge ahead on, now that the Huff piece was done. Every morning for two weeks after the acceptance letter and check came, Emmitt sat as his desk in front of the PC and tried to write. But nothing came. No flash of inspiration. Not even a glimmer of inspiration.

After the two weeks of creating nothing but empty pages, Emmitt stopped trying. He was blocked. That was all there was to it. He had been there before, and it always came to an end. He just had to wait it out was all. Fortunately, for his finances, at least, he had committed to teaching a creative writing seminar that summer at his old high school. The teaching would take his mind off his own creative troubles, the paycheck would come in handy, and by the time the seminar was over he would be back in the saddle again.

But things didn't turn out that way at all. The words did not come. If teaching the seminar helped, it didn't show. The only positive result of doing so was that at the end of it he was offered the opportunity of teaching it again the following summer. That seemed a long ways off to him—God knows anything could happen between now and then, he reasoned—but he accepted. The days passed and before he knew it he was standing up in front of that room again, addressing both new, and old faces, and hoping that this time, at the end of it, his Muse would show herself and he would be back working again at what really mattered to him.

It wasn't to be, and when the course ended he was right where he had started—blocked.

"Seems to me," Howard said when Emmitt called him one night a few days after the course ended in mid-August, "a long vacation is in order for you, my friend. A change of scenery could be just the change you need."

"Jesus, I hope so. Right now I'm wiped out."

"Any ideas on where you might take this vacation?"

"Probably Squanocket for the Derby in September. That gives me time to get things straightened out at the house. Take the phone off the hook and kick back some."

"Now you're talking. Just put the phone on the hook long enough to call and let me know where you'll be. You know, just in case I have to send along a fat royalty check'"

"Fat or thin, I need them." Then he was heading for the gate and home.

So Squanocket was the plan and one he looked forward to putting into action. But he dawdled over booking a flight. Dawdled over just about everything. He was that beat.

But one rainy night in that waning August, while looking for something to read in one of the several bookshelves scattered around the house, Emmitt came across a copy of *A Moveable Feast*. Dana had given him the book that summer they were making preparations for their upcoming Paris trip. As he pulled the book from the shelf a piece of note paper floated to the floor. Picking it up he saw written on the white page, in his wife's handwriting, a list of the things in Paris she wanted to see most of all. He took the book, the list, and a bottle of Maker's Mark out to the back porch. With the sound of the rain coming down he drank half of the bottle and re-read Hemingway's little book all the way through. Groggy as he was the next morning when he awoke, for the first time in quite a while he knew what he was going to do.

For Dana. That's what he told himself as he made his way back to the porch, this time with a mug of strong coffee. He had the list she'd prepared. Knew what she wanted. If she wasn't alive to check those items off, one by one, he was.

But he would do it for himself as well, he decided as the strong coffee took hold. God yes. Paris for himself. And from there? Maybe Spain? He was too late for Pamplona and the festival Hemingway wrote about. But there was more to Spain than bullfighting. He could go to Madrid. See the Picassos in the Prada. Go down to the coast and the beaches where he could swim and soak up the sun. He could do any damn thing he wanted. Take care of Dana's list; be done with it. Though he would not—probably never would—be done with her. Still. This trip? The rest of it could be for him.

Now, on his first night in Paris, exhausted from the flight, Emmitt lay in bed with the double windows open listening to the sounds of the bar up the street that hadn't become annoying yet.

How strange it all was, he thought as his memories of those early days with her flooded his head. His first book had come out and they had the money to go anywhere they wanted. Yet they had put off her dream until it was too late. And yes, he had to agree with her, *could* agree with her now, it was a big regret indeed.

***

The landlady, Sylvie, tall, pleasant looking with brownish hair, in her mid-thirties, wearing blue jeans, a white shirt and heeled boots with a leather satchel slung over one shoulder, stopped by the morning after he arrived. She had called first. Surprised by the ringing of the phone in the little apartment, not even aware there *was* a telephone in the apartment, Emmitt had been unsure if he should answer or not. Finally, when it wouldn't stop ringing, he hit the talk button and said, "Hello?"

"Monsieur Emmitt Raines?" he heard a female voice say on the other end.

"Yes."

"Bonjour!" the female voice on the other end continued. "It's Sylvie. Sylvie Gallant."

After getting his permission to do so, she showed up a half hour later, along with a little girl, Coralie, her daughter. It was a little awkward at first. Since Dana's death he always seemed uncomfortable around new people.

But with another energetic *Bonjour*, followed with a polite handshake, Sylvie quickly put him at ease. "Is everything okay here?" she asked, indicating the apartment with a little wave of her hand.

"Very much so," Emmitt said, as the three of them moved into the small sitting room just off the narrow entranceway.

Sylvie's daughter made herself comfortable in the little child's rocking chair in the living room. Emmitt had wondered about this chair. "Is mine," she explained, both her accent and her bright smile much like her mother's. "From when me and Mama lived here."

Though both of them spoke English better than Emmitt had expected, for being four years old, Coralie had a *really* good command of it. "Her papa," Sylvie explained, when Emmitt commented on this. "He is *Anglais*. In France, you know," she went on, "As children in school we learn your language. But Gerald gave her what you call a leg up?"

He couldn't help but laugh at the quizzical look on her face. "Yes. That's what we call it. Your Gerald gave her a very good leg up."

"Oui." But the quizzical look faded. "He's not my Gerald anymore."

Emmitt was glad when Coralie spoke up before he could say anything, to explain how her papa had taught her other things beside English. Sylvie seemed grateful for the interruption as well. Even if she put a quick end to it.

"Excuse the little one, Monsieur, she likes to talk." After a quick look around the place, and satisfied that everything was in order, she added, "And now we must go. Call me, please, if there is something you need.

"I will, definitely."

"Merci," and with another, *bonjour,* and that little wave of her hand, Sylvie and her daughter were gone.

She was nothing like Dana at all, other than that she was young, pretty, and alive, as Dana had been once. Yet after her and her daughter left, for no reason he could put his finger on, Emmitt kept thinking how his landlady *did* remind him of his wife.

Alone again, he sat in the kitchen with another cup of the rich French coffee he'd found in the cupboard. Through the open window he could hear someone in the courtyard below putting trash in the bins. Another tenant, he thought. Like him, a tourist? Or a person who lived there year round? From the front he could hear the sounds of the street, a motorbike racing up the cobblestones, a car horn blowing, perhaps a taxi sounding for its fare. When the motorbike moved further on and the car horn ceased, there came the voices of pedestrians drifting up through the wide open windows—sounds of a city all new to him. Enveloped in the sounds, it came to him why Sylvie reminded him of his dead wife. Her smile. Only that—her smile, all wide and honest as Dana's always was.

It certainly didn't take much to get him thinking about her. Just a smile on a strange woman's face that sort of seemed like Dana's.

Which brought to mind a question that sometimes nagged at him. Was there ever going to be a woman in his life? Christ, he supposed he was still young enough and healthy. At fifty-four, he was certainly not decrepit. For the most part he possessed his looks. True, his very dark hair—just like his father's his mother always said—was now streaked with gray. As well as cut short. Dana had never liked that at all, but now that she was gone he much preferred the ease of keeping it that way.

He had noticed a woman here and there in his travels, at the grocery store on whatever errand he might be involved with, looking at him. But the idea of making it something more—of exchanging an awkward smile, of striking up a conversation—was something he couldn't bring himself to pursue. He just couldn't imagine himself with any woman but Dana. Whether he had certain needs or not was beside the point. He could take care of those needs on his own.

He stood up from the little table and took his empty coffee cup to the sink. Another motorbike raced up the street out front. The little guttural roar of its engines faded, replaced by the sound of a work truck's warning beeps as it went into reverse. What was it his grandfather had always said when it was time to get going? *We're burning daylight here.* Yes, that he was, Emmitt thought. Burning daylight to no good end. It was time to get on with it. To see what Paris had to offer him for the day, to check off the things on Dana's list.

Between the landlady's visit and his lingering over coffee it was close to eleven before Emmitt made it down to the street. The morning was mild, a light wind blowing, only a few high wispy clouds in an otherwise blue sky. In khaki slacks and a long-sleeved shirt he was comfortable as he walked down the steep cobblestoned street to the corner where he turned right and headed up the Rue des Abbesses.

The street traffic was one way and crowded with unfamiliar little European cars. The sidewalks on either side of the street were crowded as well, with people hurrying along in both directions. Some had shopping bags in their hands, the ends of fresh unwrapped baguettes sticking out from the top. Others held onto plastic shopping bags, the labels of various trendy shops shining brightly in the late morning sun. Lines of people waited their turn in the *boulangeries* and *boucheries* and other groceries that dotted the busy avenue. Not only that, it seemed on every corner he came to there was some sort of café where people sat outside at little tables just off the sidewalk, drinking coffee, beer, or wine, and smoking cigarettes while watching the world go by. It was as if all of Montmartre was on the move with people going about their daily business—Emmitt a part of it, too, just another human being on the move, different because he was but a visitor, one of many other Americans out and about in the flow.

After several blocks the road forked. In the island created by this fork there was a restaurant with the church-like name *Le Basilica* in unpretentious scroll on a sign above its doors. Emmitt stopped to read the menu posted on a glassed-in board out front, happy to see that it was in both French and English. The dish of the day was a duck cassoulet and though he had no idea what that might be, it sounded good and he decided to come back that evening for dinner. Having made this decision he headed off on the fork to the right.

Here the street was cobblestoned again, the going steadily uphill. As he walked, Emmitt left behind the crowds of automobile traffic and people below. Rising up from the sidewalks on both sides were the four and five story apartment buildings that seemed to make up the Montmartre he had seen so far. The paint of the pale plaster fronts was faded, over how much time he couldn't know. Balconies faced the street, protected by the same sort of iron grillwork he was familiar with from the apartment. Most of these balconies were decorated with flowerboxes, the flowers blooming in the sunlight and hiding the French doors that led inside.

Looking up once as he walked along the quiet street, he was just in time to see a tabby cat, perched on the iron grill of one apartment, leap to the balcony of the next. Emmitt's heart stopped in momentary suspense until the cat landed safely, disappeared from view.

He came to an intersection where a windmill rose up from the sidewalk. *Moulin Radat,* according to the bronze plaque on the base of the windmill. *Moulin Radat* was one of two working windmills left in Montmartre, Emmitt read, warmed now by the sunlight streaming into the intersection of the two streets, light reflecting off the big wooden blades that rotated only slightly, the breeze wafting along the street barely enough to push them.

Down from the windmill on the corner of another intersection there was one of those little brown tourist information signs that were posted throughout Paris. Sacre Coeur, Emmitt read as he came closer. A white arrow below the printed information pointed down the street to his right. Sacre Coeur wasn't on Dana's list. But he was curious, and for the first time in his walk that morning Emmitt had a destination.

The street—cobblestoned like so many of them in Montmartre—led him down, and then up into a square crowded with tourists, art galleries, cafes, Nutella take-out stands, and street artists, their easels set up and ready to sketch or paint one's portrait for a small fee. After pushing his way through the crowds, ignoring the street artists and beggars who tried to stop him, he came around a corner where a massive cathedral rose up, white and gleaming, into the cloudless sky above Paris.

Sacre Coeur was certainly impressive enough, Emmitt thought. Archways carved into the stone walls held stained glass windows reflecting the sunlight pouring through them. Flanking the three large entranceways into the church were two iron sculptures of men on horseback, their arms outstretched as if they were waving to the crowd of people below. A bell tower rose from the top of the structure, surrounded by smaller similar domes, all of them topped off with crosses. As Emmitt strained his neck to see all the way up, the bells began to ring the hour, the clarion sound pealing out, over all of Paris it seemed.

Impressive as all this was from below, what he liked even more was the view from the top of the stairs once he made the climb. It couldn't have been more than 75 degrees, the air fresh and cool—free as it was from the buildings of the city hemming it in. It felt good against his skin after the exertion of making it up all those steps. Stretched out below were the twisting streets of Montmartre. Rising up from them—just as the beautiful church rose up behind Emmitt—all the roofs of Paris were gleaming, some bright, some dull, in the sunlight streaming down out of the cloudless sky. And far away, off to the right, the Eiffel Tower stood, lone iron sentinel standing watch over the city.

He turned to go inside the cathedral but was blocked by a dark-skinned teenage girl thrusting a clipboard at him. When he tried to go around her, she covered first an ear and then her mouth. Seeing that he still didn't understand, she pointed again at the clipboard. The paper attached there, written first in French, then English, then in Spanish, requested: Please Help the Deaf Mute Children of Paris. Below this the paper held a list of names, email addresses, and the amounts of the donation given.

"Okay," he said. "I understand now," and though the girl couldn't hear him she smiled and nodded her head.

Where they stood, just in front of the main entrance way into the cathedral, the people coming up the stairs had to go around them. *Like a stream breaking against a boulder in the middle of its flow.* It was a silly thought, which probably came from the writer in him. He signed his name in the appropriate column, by-passed the email address slot, wrote down one euro in the donation column, and handed the coin to the girl.

She looked briefly at the euro in her hand, and then shook her head. For a deaf mute, Emmitt decided, she was certainly good at getting her point across. When he smiled and began to walk away the girl grabbed at his shirt.

At that moment a young Frenchman, in his twenties, wearing jeans, a blue T-shirt and a Boston Red Sox cap, came up and pulled the girl away.

"She's only a gypsy," the young man said. "Working a scam."

"Really?" Though he wasn't that surprised, Emmitt did find it kind of sad.

"Oui. She can hear and talk as well as you and I. There's a whole gang of them."

The young man waved his hand around. When Emmitt looked, sure enough there were several other girls, much like the one the Frenchman still held onto, the same kind of clipboards in their hands.

"This one, I know," the young Frenchman continued. "She's here during the day. At night she works in Clichy." The motions he made with his hands left little doubt as to the nature of the work she did at night.

This must have been true and more than she could take, for the girl turned and spat in the young Frenchman's face. Laughing, he pushed her away, casually wiped his face, and said, "See?"

"Oui. I do," Emmitt said. "Merci. Thank you very much."

"It's okay, my friend. It's only my duty. These thieving gypsies make it difficult for honest entrepreneurs like myself."

He held out one of those little plastic replicas of the famous cathedral Emmitt had noticed others hawking to the tourists. Both the young Frenchman's smile and the white statue in his hand gleamed in the sunlight. Emmitt laughed, shook his head, and bought the trinket from the youth, figuring it was the least he could do. He watched as the young man walked away along the top of the steps, stopping long enough to blow a kiss at the gypsy girl, who had joined her friends. She gave him the finger in return. With his laughter drifting out behind him, the young Frenchman moved on.

He'd had enough. Enough of sightseeing for one day. Instead of going inside the cathedral as he'd planned, he consulted the fold-out tourist map he'd brought with him and headed off toward the apartment.

He wasn't as far away as he'd thought. After walking not more than ten minutes —all downhill, he was happy to find—he came to the café in the square at the top of rue Ravignan. Not yet four o'clock in the afternoon, there were plenty of empty tables out front. Emmitt sat at one tucked away in a corner in the back. Here he would have a good view of the street below and the people coming and going. He had every intention of ordering a coffee and a bottle of spring water. But when the waiter came Emmitt ordered a Heineken instead.

The beer was cold and refreshing, just the pick-me-up he needed. So much so that he finished it quicker than he expected to and signaled the waiter for another. As the waiter was setting the fresh beer and glass down, Emmitt noticed a movement out of the corner of his eye. A woman, alone and carrying a shopping bag, sat down at the table at the end of his row. Like most of the women he had seen so far in Paris, this one was stylishly dressed, a bright red scarf around her neck setting off her ensemble. After arranging her things the woman turned to find the waiter, saw Emmitt, and gave him a smile that took him away for just a moment. A man appeared suddenly, bounding down the steps from the square behind the café. He joined the woman, she waved a gloved hand at the waiter—and the moment was gone.

As it had been in front of the cathedral when the young Frenchman laughed his way through the crowd of tourists and hucksters, it was enough for Emmitt. He paid his tab and walked the short block down to the apartment.

***

On the Metro to the Louvre the next day Emmitt realized he was feeling like his old self again. Not as alive, say, as he had been before the onset of Dana's illness. Or that morning at the Cut on Squanocket. But he was awake, and aware, and excited about the adventure he was on for the day. A good meal the night before, followed by a sound sleep, along with the rambling walk through Montmartre, had done away with his jet lag. As the train pulled into the station for the museum, Emmitt was the first one out of his seat and waiting for the doors to open.

But the long halls of religious art from the Middle Ages and beyond did nothing for him. When he finally reached the Mona Lisa he was disappointed as well. The throngs of people all wanting to view the little painting took a lot from it. On his way out he came upon the Winged Victory of Samothrace. The way the statue first came into view—at the top of a long, wide marble staircase, with the light from a window overhead shining down—took Emmitt's breath away. This was more like it, he thought. He stayed there looking up at the ancient sculpture, oblivious to the people around him going up the stairs. For Emmitt it did not matter. He wanted to stay right where he was until he had his fill.

On the way back to Montmartre he decided he was glad there was only the one museum on Dana's list. The next item up was the Eiffel Tower, followed by Notre Dame. The Arc de Triumph, and the cemetery, Pere Lachaise, were the last two on the list. He figured by the end of the week he would be able to cross these off as well. It wasn't on her list, but Emmitt knew there was no way he was leaving Paris without a visit to Shakespeare & Company, the bookstore on the Left Bank, where Hemingway and Joyce had gotten their start. He would be done, then, with being a tourist. The rest of the time he spent in Paris would involve long walks, good food, and enjoying the fact that he was there.

There alive, was his sudden thought as the train rolled to a stop at the Abbesses station. Yes, unlike Dana, who had wanted to go so badly. And just like that, his brief realization only moments before of how her absence wasn't quite so troubling, seemed so very wrong for him to have.

Good old fashioned guilt. Would he ever fully let it go, he wondered as he waited for the elevator to the street. If he was anything like his mother—who had blamed herself damn near forever for not doing enough to prevent his father from killing himself—then, no, Emmitt would not.

His father was there, then, a man Emmitt hadn't considered for a long time. Not until he thought of his mother. He had hated the man for so long, beginning as a boy when he discovered the truth about the man and his death that day in his mother's bedroom. That hatred had stayed with him well into his twenties. Until marrying Dana and being happy had pushed that hatred deep into the background. Not brought up again until the letter from Eileen and its startling news. And again when Dana was pregnant for the first time and he confessed his fears to Howard about being a father—since he was one who had no example to learn from. Fortunately, time and his life that followed, had allowed that hate to slip away. Now, here it was. Along with the question, shouldn't that hate not be replaced by guilt?

His mother had found a happiness late in her life. A happiness, as best he knew, free of that old guilt. Found this happiness by marrying her boss, the mayor, some forty odd years after the loss of her first husband. And though it was true that she and the mayor were together for only two years, before an automobile accident in Tallahassee took their lives, Emmitt's mother had been happy as he had never really known her to be before.

So there was a chance for him, too.

When the elevator doors opened, he followed the other people in the lift with him up the short flight of steps and through a turnstile. Suddenly he was out on the street. The rain of the morning had gone, the sun was out, a soft breeze blew along the rue de Abbesses, and he *was* alive and that was all there was to it.

*****

Finally he had checked off the items on Dana's list. And he had been to the places *he* wanted to see as well—Shakespeare & Company, the building in Montparnasse that Hemingway and Hadley and the baby Bumby lived in above the sawmill, Harry's Bar where he had a couple of drinks, the bookstalls along the Left Bank. Feeling he had done his best to honor his wife as well as satisfying his own curiosity, Emmitt decided he could use an evening of extravagant entertainment.

On the Wednesday night of his second week in Paris, wearing his one pair of dress slacks and a corduroy blazer, Emmitt found himself at the Moulin Rouge following the maître'd to his seat. This turned out to be at a little round table in a terraced section off from the main floor where the dinner guests sat. Two women were already seated there. After pulling out a chair for him, the maître de bowed at the three of them and disappeared into the rapidly-filling cabaret. At first Emmitt thought the women might be sisters.

"Monsieur Raines," the one he presumed to be the older of the two sisters said as he sat down. "This is a surprise."

He didn't understand, and it must have showed on his face.

"It's Sylvie," and she placed her hand on his wrist. "The apartment?"

"I didn't recognize you," he said, embarrassed that he didn't. After all, that morning when the landlady and her little daughter came to meet him wasn't that long ago. "Sorry about that."

Her pleasant laugh, followed with that little wave of her hand he remembered from the other morning, indicated there was nothing for him to be sorry for.

"A coincidence, perhaps? Running into one another here?"

"Very much so."

"This is a friend of mine from America, here to visit." Remembering that they were not alone, Sylvie lifted her hand from Emmitt's wrist to put it on her companion's. "Monsieur Raines is staying in my apartment, Leila. The one you liked so much when you were here last."

"Emmitt is fine," he said as he reached across the table to take the hand offered to him. "Nice to meet you."

Sylvie's laugh and smile were a pleasure, he realized above the bright lights and the bustle of the famous nightclub. Pleasures, female laughter and smiles, he hadn't enjoyed in a while.

A complimentary bottle of champagne in an ice bucket came with the table. Emmitt filled their glasses, Sylvie stopping him when hers was three-quarters full. Sitting back with his champagne Emmitt observed his companions. It was easy enough, for Sylvie had turned back to her friend and apparently picked up the conversation they had been sharing before Emmitt arrived. She did it in a way that did not seem rude at all. One of the many mysteries of women he most likely would never fully comprehend, Emmitt decided as he poured more champagne into his glass.

The two women were very attractive. Leila, in an American sort of way, Sylvie in that more sophisticated manner he had noticed in Parisian women. Leila looked to be in her late twenties, with a round face and sharp green eyes. The eyes went well with her hair, red and long, in a French braid that hung almost to her waist. Something struck Emmitt as a little unnatural about her eyes. They shone with a glint in the light of the room. Contact lenses, he thought.

Sylvie Gallant was another story, one he suddenly wanted to know more about. Her skin, that naturally olive tone some women had, along with her olive face and soft dark eyes—well, one couldn't help but pay attention. Her brown hair cut just above her neckline framed her face very well. He remembered now from her visit at the apartment that Sylvie was a tall woman, almost as tall as him. Remembered too, how after she left he had dwelled on her smile, and the way it reminded him of Dana's.

Here at the Moulin Rouge, Sylvie looked fantastic. In a silky red dress with a high neck and long sleeves open at the shoulders, and silver chain earrings dangling against her neck, she looked like no other woman he had ever been with. And here was a surprising thought: he wondered what that would be like? Being *with* her. Fortunately, before he could go any further with these thoughts, the lights dimmed, a tuxedo-wearing emcee strolled out on the center stage, and the show began.

For the next hour Emmitt was witness to a spectacle of music, light, dance, bare flesh, sequined costumes, and exotic headdresses, weaving dangerously atop the can-can girls as they sang and kicked their legs up on any one of the three stages. Tacky and overdone, funny—even if he didn't understand the jokes the French comedians told. Sad as well when one of the female entertainers in a black evening dress took center stage and sang a mournful ballad. It was one hell of a show, and he was glad he had followed through on his whim and bought a ticket for the night's entertainment. The two women only added to his enjoyment.

"Awesome! Thanks for suggesting this, Sylvie," Leila said at intermission. Instead of going outside with the others when the lights went up, the three of them stayed at their table and started on the fresh bottle of champagne Leila had ordered. The girl's green eyes were even sharper with her enjoyment of the spectacle. "I needed a night out, after all those hostels."

"Leila's been backpacking her way across the Continent," Sylvie told Emmitt. "She spent her nights at youth hostels along her way."

"That sounds like fun," Emmitt said. "A great way to see the country."

"Leila had lots of fun. Some of it perhaps not what her parents would approve of. Or her boyfriend back home. Especially in Madrid."

"Sylvie," the girl protested.

"It's just I am a little jealous," Sylvie continued. "Since Gerald decided I was too old, too ugly, anymore. My love life? What can I say?"

And then there was that wide open smile Emmitt remembered form the morning at the apartment. The smile that reminded him of Dana's.

"Well," she continued. "Perhaps I should go to Madrid."

"I doubt you'd have to go that far," Emmitt said as he topped off their champagne glasses. The champagne must have been getting to him a little, considering what he said next. "An attractive woman such as yourself."

"Oh?" Sylvie turned then, putting the full force of that smile on him. "You find me attractive then, Emmitt? How nice of you." Putting her hand on his she repeated, "How very nice of you."

"Well, isn't this night getting more interesting by the minute," Leila laughed.

"I'll drink to that," he said, and the three of them raised their glasses to one another.

In the little bit of time left in the intermission, Leila managed to tell of her recent travels, beginning with how she left New York in mid-August and flew to Rome. From Rome she had backpacked down to Pompeii to see the ruins. She hadn't taken into consideration the fact that August is the very hottest month in Europe. Because of the high temperatures and humid air she bought a rail pass and took the train to the Isle of Capri. She swam in the Med, took a tourist boat into the Blue Grotto, and then worked her way back up through Italy to Spain, either hiking or riding the Eurorail. At night she stayed in youth hostels.

"Where you met some hotties," Sylvie interjected with a laugh.

"Only the one!" But Leila laughed, too.

After Paris she was flying home to finish her thesis and last year of grad school in New York. "It's been a great trip," Leila concluded. "But I'll be glad to get home."

"Even with your parents?" Sylvie asked. "You seemed not to enjoy their company so much when the three of you stayed at my apartment."

"Your apartment is very small for three adults," Leila said. "I was younger then. Besides, what twenty year old girl wants to be in Paris with her mom and dad?"

Emmitt enjoyed Leila's frank version of her travels almost as much as he had the first half of the show. He was also grateful that so far neither woman had asked too much about him. Once, during a lull in Leila's narrative, Sylvie had turned to him, but just as she was about to say something Leila started up again. Then the lights dimmed in the cabaret again and Emmitt was off the hook.

The third bottle of champagne seemed to slow him down, to cause a throbbing just above his temples. Emmitt was glad when the show ended and the lights went up. Before he knew it he was standing out on the sidewalk in front of the cabaret with Leila and Sylvie, breathing in the fresh air of the night while the rest of the show-goers milled around them, jumped into waiting cabs, or walked down the busy boulevard to disappear in the lights of the city.

"I'm free Friday night, Emmitt," Sylvie said, her hand on his wrist again. "Perhaps you'd like to have dinner with me?"

Before Emmitt could reply Leila took Sylvie's arm and steered her into the crosswalk at the intersection. He watched as the two women crossed the boulevard to the Metro station on the other side. A prostitute, tall and leggy, crossed the street behind them. She was wearing a red dress and her hair—an even brighter shade of red than her dress—fell over the scarf around her neck. He thought of Sylvie and her invitation. Would he take her up on it, he wondered. Why not make it easy on himself, less complicated all the way around, and just go with the prostitute, whose invitation was for all and sundry with the money to be her companion for the night?

Having no answer to these questions, he walked back up the long hill of rue Lepic toward the Abbesses and the apartment.

***

So now, here he was, with Sylvie Gallant, a complete stranger to him until only two nights back. Arm in arm they walked along the wide and busy rue St. Lazare, turning toward the river when they came to rue de

Caumartin. The sidewalks on both sides of the boulevard were crowded with people out and about after the rains earlier in the week. The night air was clean and cool, marred only by the occasional exhaust fumes of a bus or truck roaring by.

Three blocks down from her apartment they crossed a wide intersection. Off to the left a church rose up from the park like grounds surrounding it. No light came from inside the ancient, gothic looking building. A spire with a thin cross topped the church, the white of the spire and cross gleaming in the lights of the city.

A young couple sat on a bench in the courtyard before the church. They were kissing, engrossed in one another, oblivious to the city and the people going by. In the light reflected by the church's spire and cross Emmitt could see an expectant smile on Sylvie's face.

"Young lovers," she said, her brown eyes on his, "enjoying a beautiful evening."

"Paris is the city of love, is it not?"

"You sound a little cynical." She stepped back from him. Maybe because they had heard talking, or finally noticed the city life going on around them, the young couple got up from the bench and strolled away hand in hand. "Have you ever been in love, Emmitt?"

"A couple of times. Long ago."

"But you can still remember?" And there was that smile that reminded him in a way of Dana. "How it was to be in love?"

"Very much so," he said, hoping she didn't hear the sudden ache in his voice.

One more block and they came to the restaurant Sylvie had chosen for the evening. This was a small bistro, across the boulevard from the Café de la Paix, and down from the opera house at the other end of the square.

"Here we are," Sylvie said as Emmitt held the door open for her. "My choice for tonight."

"I thought you might be taking us to the Café de la Paix when we first came around the corner" Emmitt replied while they waited for a maître d' to seat them. "It's in all the guidebooks as a good place to go."

"Yes, it is a good place to go—for tourists. I like this place better."

"Then I'm sure I will like it better, too."

When he smiled Sylvia laughed again. The maître d' was there then to lead them to a table. Even if it turned out to be in a corner the table still had a good view. Not that it mattered—in the small dining area all the tables had a good view of the square outside, where the more famous Café de la Paix and the opera house dominated the scene. The light inside was soft and comfortable. The bistro, though small, was very busy, the staff harried but professional as they moved.

"If you like we could go to the tourist place across the street another time." She unfolded her white cloth napkin and placed it in her lap below the equally very white tablecloth. "The food *is* good there."

Before he could say anything the waiter was there for their drink order—wine for Sylvie and for Emmitt a bourbon and water. He was glad she hadn't wanted champagne like they drank at the Moulin Rouge. He would have certainly agreed if she had, despite the way he had felt the next morning, headachy and queasy and wishing he had passed on the third bottle.

"What about the opera?" he asked when the waiter left, and in an attempt to make some sort of small talk with this woman he did not know. "Have you been?"

"Once, actually, before I was married." She paused, her hands messing with the napkin in her lap. "It's funny you ask about the opera. The one time I went was with Gerald. Our first date. I was working at the bank, then. A teller, planning to work my way up. He was a broker with a London firm that did business with our bank. I suppose he wanted to impress me with the opera."

"Did he? "

"Not with the opera. With everything else, yes. He did impress me. A mistake I have paid for."

"You seem to be doing fine, now," Emmitt said quickly. The dismissive waive of her hand said that she didn't want to talk about her ex-husband and might be heading that way in spite of herself.

"It took some time. My work at the bank led me into real estate. Which, luckily, I seem to be a natural. And of course, I am a mother now and must do fine."

They were interrupted for a moment by the waiter with their drinks. Both were quiet as they took their first polite sips, Emmitt touching the rim of his cocktail glass to hers before he did.

"We never got around to it the other night," she said. "I suppose from the fun we were having. But what do you do Emmitt? For work. "

The bourbon was hot and strong, cooled only a little by the water and ice. After swallowing the first long sip, he waited a moment to let it burn all the way down to his stomach.

"I'm a writer."

How clear and real that seemed suddenly and that hadn't in a while.

"Ah, like my grandmother's friend, Camus."

"Sort of, I suppose, though not in quite that exalted sphere. I mean, I don't think my work will be required reading in the schools like his."

It was funny, but no matter how long he had worked at his chosen profession, through the successes and the failures and the in-between, he could never shake the uncomfortable feeling that came over him when others wanted to discuss his work with him.

Saving him for the moment, the waiter reappeared to take their meal order—onion soup to begin, followed by pepper steak for Sylvie, oysters and Sole Menieres for Emmitt. Then, beyond the droning of the conversations around them, and the soft sound of Parisian pop music coming through speakers hidden somewhere in the walls, it was quiet at their table.

"What books have you written?" Sylvie asked, breaking the uneasy silence. "Perhaps I've read them."

Taking another sip of his drink Emmitt decided to ignore the discomfort and get on with it.

"I hope so. I can use all the royalties I can get."

The two of them laughed over this, Emmitt's awkwardness fading some with the laughter as they finished their cocktails. With Sylvie's nodding approval Emmitt signaled to their waiter for another round.

"The one that got my career started was called *Three Men*," he said.

"The title has me curious," Sylvie said.

"I feel strange saying it, but it was a good book."

It *was* a good book. And big—something most young writer's first books tended to be, Howard Kamen had told him. A book difficult for him to explain, especially now, with all the time that had passed since he'd written it.

"It was well reviewed," he continued, "by the critics that counted—or so my agent said. It even sold some copies. The second book, *River*, was not so well reviewed but sold much better. Probably because there was more sex in it. It's a funny business."

"I wish I had read them."

It was nice how the look on her face was so sincere. Seeing her smile like that took away whatever discomfort within him still remained.

"Financially, my saving grace were the films made from those books," Emmitt continued. "A very popular actor played the lead in both. It was funny how that man's career took off after being in those films. They were both very bad. And didn't advance my own career the way I'd have liked."

"That is sad, of course. But how life is sometimes."

"Oh yes. Fortunately my wife's job was stable. She taught art at the local college. We had some roughs times in the beginning. And my books sold all right. Even if there were no more movies I was still able to publish and make somewhat of a living."

"Your wife?"

He saw how she looked at his hands then, at the finger of his left. The ring was resting in the top drawer of his bureau at home, back in the little box it had come in almost thirty years before.

"Yes. Passed away a little over two years ago."

"Any children?"

"No. No kids."

"I'm sorry to hear that."

"Yeah," Emmitt said. "We weren't lucky in that department. Not like you, with your little Coralie."

"Yes," she said, "I am very lucky."

He did not go on to say how the fact of his sorrow—his loss—at the death of his wife was why he was in Paris. And why, directly or not, he was having dinner with this beautiful woman in a French restaurant he would never have thought to go to on his own.

"I'll have to make a point of looking for your books," Sylvie said. "Perhaps Amazon has them. Or Shakespeare & Company."

"Amazon perhaps. Doubtful at the other, sad to say. I'll send you a copy."

"Signed?"

"Of course."

Then the waiter appeared with their dinner and for a while the food occupied their full attention. It was a good meal, the woman and the setting adding to it immensely. During dinner at one point he asked Sylvie if it were true that the Eiffel Tower had some sort of sparkly light show going on after dark. She told him this was true, that if he wished they could go there after dinner. He said that he *did* wish and when they finished with the meal, had coffee, and brandy after, he hailed one of the taxis waiting in the queue across from the restaurant. They were quiet in the back seat of the cab during the drive through the city, though strangely enough—to Emmitt at least—they held hands as if it were the most natural thing in the world.

But sitting next to her in the cab, he suddenly had the godawful thought that it was all wrong. He should be in that cab, going to see the Eiffel Tower at night with all the lights, with Dana.

The taxi came to a stop and brought him back to the present. In another moment they were out on the street beneath the base of the famous tower, all iron and gridwork and lit up by hundreds upon hundreds of shimmering lights as it rose into the night sky over the city.

"The view is better from back there," Sylvie said, pointing at the Ecole Militaire behind them, all white and shining on the hill at the top of the Champs du Mars. "But only in the daytime. Too many pickpockets, or worse even, at night."

"We won't take the chance then." He was more aware of her body, close to his like that, than he really wanted to be. "The view is fine from right here."

Sylvie shivered in the cool breeze he could feel coming up from the river. "You're cold. Here, take my jacket," he said.

"It's all right. Let's go back my apartment."

"Should we walk? It's not that far, and the walk will warm you."

"No," she said. "Let's get a taxi."

But back at her place, the taxi's engine idling as Sylvie got out and Emmitt paid the fare, when he went to follow her he told the driver not to leave.

"It's been a very pleasant evening, Sylvie," he told her out on the sidewalk.

"But?"

"I know this sounds funny. But I think I'd better say goodnight."

"Are you sure?"

"No, I'm not," he said. "But I think so."

"I'm sorry you feel that way, Emmitt." She smiled. Or tried to. When she went to kiss him goodnight, it was not on his lips, as earlier, but on his cheek. "Bonsoir."

He could hear the disappointment in her voice. For a second he wondered what was wrong with him that he was not letting the cab go and following her up to her apartment. There was no way to tell her that his dead wife had ridden all the way back to the apartment with them. Dana had been there, that determined look on her face, her declaration, *That's it, Emmitt, We're going to Paris, no matter what.* No, he couldn't tell Sylvie any of this. He could only do what he had to right then, and that was to leave.

He called her the next day. Not sure what he would say when she answered, part of him hoped it would be her voicemail instead. Leaving a message would be so much easier, and then he would be done with it.

"I'm sorry about last night," he managed, when instead of voicemail, Sylvie *did* answer.

"Don't be." Her voice sounded a little restrained, though that could only have been his imagination. "It was a nice evening."

"I meant after."

"Emmitt, I understand. You are not ready. It took me a long time after Gerald left. I can imagine a death must be even harder. At least with divorce you can tell yourself you are getting your payback on him. Or her."

Her easy laughter over the phone settled the matter for him and they ended the conversation with mutual promises of staying in touch. He knew they wouldn't though and it was too bad. She was a beautiful and interesting woman and he would have liked the chance to get to know her better. The chance to see where things between them might go.

But like she told him over the phone—he wasn't ready.

Two days later, on Monday morning, he boarded the train out of Paris. For Spain, and whatever might happen there.

Part Four: Blue Waters

Emmitt had no set itinerary when he boarded the train in Paris. After buying a rail pass at the station he looked up the schedules for Pamplona. To get there he would have to change trains in San Sebastian, the coastal town on the other side of the Pyrenees. It wasn't his intention when he boarded the train that morning, but on a whim, after the train rolled into the station in San Sebastian, smelling the clean salt air of the Atlantic Ocean while stretching his legs on the platform, Emmitt decided to stay. Why not? He was running on no schedule these days. But doing what he liked, when and where he wanted to do it. The ocean was there. He could smell it in the air, clean and refreshing, and just what the doctor ordered after his stay in the crowded and noisy city of Paris. He would get a room at a hotel, swim in the ocean, and enjoy good seafood. Maybe find a guide who could take him up into the Pyrenees for some trout fishing on one of the clear mountain streams he had seen from the train window as they climbed up and down out of the mountains. When he'd had his fill he'd move on to Pamplona.

The hotel room, the swimming in the ocean, and the good seafood, all worked out fine. The only bust was the fishing. There were no guides in San Sebastian and apparently logging operations in the mountains had silted the nearest river and killed the fish. It was a shame but there wasn't anything he could do about it. After two days of the ocean and the food he was back on the train.

It was mid-week when he arrived in Pamplona, no festivals were going on, and Emmitt wasn't able to see a bullfight. Instead, he walked around the old town, explored the fortifications left over from the days of the Romans, and made his way down the cobblestoned streets where the bulls ran during the festival of San Fermin that Hemingway had made famous. He managed to find the hotel bar where the writer and his companions had drunk between bullfights, and got pleasantly buzzed one hot afternoon his second day there. That night he ate a delicious rabbit stew in a quaint Spanish restaurant in the square down from that hotel. The next morning he headed on to Madrid.

His first night in the city he had a late dinner in one of the many cafes surrounding Plaza Mayor and watching, as he ate, the town come alive.

Men and women dressed to the nines moved from one café, or shop, to another while music—folk, rock, and flamenco, performed by street musicians—filled the air. The next day Emmitt went to the Prada, and when he was done with the Goyas and the Velequez paintings, went down the block to the Museo Reina Sofia to see Picasso's *Guernica* on exhibit. Afterwards, he spent the rest of the afternoon walking in a big park not far from the museum, the sounds of the city muted by the trees and shrubbery, and where young couples sat on blankets by the banks of a small lake, drinking wine, smoking cigarettes, laughing, and making out. Picasso's painting about the Spanish Civil War was much on his mind as he walked, trying to picture how the city had been then, under constant fire and full of the dead. If not for the fact the next day was Sunday and he had tickets for the bullfights, Emmitt would have left Madrid, satisfied he had gotten out of that city all he needed to.

Like Picasso's *Guernica*, the bullfight stayed with Emmitt all that Sunday night as he dabbled with tapas and Spanish Madeira in a bar just off of the Plaza Mayor. The music, the crowds, the matadors in their *Suits of Light*, the majestic strength of the bulls as they ran and wheeled on the sand … Emmitt couldn't put out of his head. The ancient spectacle of life and death, bravery and fear, color and music, played out on a warm afternoon in an arena.

The only regret Emmitt had while there, was that Dana wasn't with him to see it all—a regret followed just as quickly by the knowledge that the death of the bulls would have bothered her—that her being upset might have colored his joy in being there.

The remembrance brought Emmitt up short. As he signaled to the waiter for another glass of wine, he realized that it had been the first time he'd thought of her since leaving Paris. Whether it was the night out with Sylvie, Dana's ghost in the cab with them on the ride back to her apartment, or something Sylvie said to him on the phone the next day, he could not say. But something had changed inside him— something very freeing of all that had gone before. He wasn't going back to Paris. Wasn't going to call Sylvie for another date. The freedom he suddenly felt was not of that kind. But he was going to do something.

***

On the way to Cannes there was an hour layover in Marseilles where many of the passengers who had filled the cars in Madrid disembarked. When the train finally pulled away from the city, Emmitt headed for the club car.

The club car was clean and well lit, mainly from the natural light of the afternoon streaming through the windows. Along with snacks and drinks, a limited supply of newspapers and magazines was available. Emmitt bought a Becks and a copy of the *Tribune* from the young bartender and took a seat in the booth nearest the bar. The beer was rich and cold, the news in the paper a mix of bad and good. Just what he felt he needed at the time.

But it didn't take long for him to put the paper down and stare out at the changed landscape—the seascape, really—they were traveling past. For after leaving the slums on the outskirts of Marseilles behind, the view was of a steep rocky coastline falling down to the Mediterranean, clear and blue and shimmering in the afternoon light as it stretched away from the shore.

Looking out at the water and the coast he realized he was glad to be out of Madrid. And Paris before that. There was no way around the fact that as amazing and beautiful as both were, in the end they were just big cities. Different, true, from the others he'd spent time in—New York, and Boston, and L.A—but still cities.

Mainly why he stayed in Florida. And not just for where he lived, the older, original part of Ft. Lauderdale, where the streets were quiet, lined with palms, sea grape trees, the houses with deep water canals behind them leading out to New River, the inlet, and the Atlantic Ocean beyond—but for the ocean. He knew that if the ocean were not there he would have left his hometown a long ago. For him the best time to go was in the early morning, just as the sun was coming up and he could have the beach and water to himself. Before tourists, and when school was out in the summer, noisy teenagers would have taken over, ruining the natural serenity Emmitt found there. After swimming out to where it was well over his head, he liked to turn over on his back and float with his eyes closed, the sun on his eyelids and the currents of the sea flowing beneath him—liked how it was all just for him. When Dana had been alive she went with him more often than not. Yet even her death hadn't taken away the magic of the salt water for him. The way it seemed to cleanse him. How even when he was out of the water, the dried sea salt sticking to his skin, he still felt clean.

Suddenly, with the train clacking noisily along the rails running the coastline of the south of France, Emmitt realized with a start that he was homesick.

Good Lord. Homesick like some kid sent off to summer camp for the first time. Even worse. Homesick for a home that hadn't seemed like much of one for quite some time.

A woman was sitting in a booth down and across from him. Other than her, the bartender, and Emmitt, the club car was empty. He had noticed her when he first came into the car—the back of her head at any rate—the light blonde hair falling over her shoulders. To rid himself of the sudden homesickness he looked up from the paper and his beer and noticed the woman again.

She was engrossed in the book on the table in front of her. But she picked that moment to look up and see Emmitt studying her. She smiled, and instead of looking away, held his gaze. Embarrassed to be caught staring like that, he was the one who turned away.

He was glad he had the beer to hide his discomfort. When he felt it safe he looked up again. The woman was lost once more in her book. Whatever opportunity held out by her to a stranger on a train, the door opened slightly with her gracious smile, was gone now.

As the train pulled into another of the small stations along the way, the woman put the book down to look out the window. She must have sensed him watching for she turned, smiled again, and said, "Hello."

Deciding he had nothing to lose, Emmitt said, "Must be a good book you're reading."

"Yes, it is." The woman smiled—an honest and unaffected smile. *Tender is the Night*. An oldie but goody. Do you know it?"

"Fitzgerald. A good book indeed." He was pleasantly surprised. Without seeing the cover of the book he had just assumed it would be one of those silly "beach reads" that always seemed to occupy the No. 1 spot on the bestseller lists. "Better than *Gatsby* I always felt. Plenty of decadent behavior and the follies of those with money and those without. Something F. Scott knew a lot about."

She laughed, a festive trilling laugh that sounded perfect for the setting: a train rolling along the coast of Southern France, two strangers making polite conversation in an otherwise empty club car in the middle of the day.

"I haven't read *The Great Gatsb*, since high school," she said. "My sister insisted I read this, since a lot of the story takes place where'll we be staying. Though I seriously doubt we'll indulge in any of the decadent behavior you mentioned."

Emboldened by her laugh Emmitt stood up, crossed the aisle, and sat at her booth.

"I wouldn't recommend it," he said. "The decadent behavior. Not unless you have plenty of money. Of course, money isn't a prerequisite for strange behavior. But I'm told it helps. Makes it easier to get out of the jams."

Then they were both laughing. For some reason Emmitt felt like something had been lifted from him—something heavy and unexplainable—but no matter, for he was in to the day now, and happy to be there.

"So you're going to Cap D'Antibes, I take it?" Emmitt asked. "It's been a while since I read the book, but I believe that's where it takes place. The French scenes at least."

"We'll be in Antibes. Just not out on the point. My sister said the Cap is too far away from everything. She rented a house just outside of the city for the late summer and fall."

"I've never been to Antibes, or the Cap. This is my first time in France, actually. I'll be staying in Cannes."

He heard the automated voice coming over the train's intercom system as it did every time they approached a station. *Cannes. Five minutes. Cannes. Next stop, Golfe Juan.* The robotic voice sounded so strange in French, but strange or not he couldn't ignore what it said.

"Speaking of which, that's me," he added.

The woman laughed, her blue eyes lit up with humor. "Well, it's certainly been nice chatting with you. Who knows? Maybe I'll bump into you in Cannes. We stayed there last year. The beaches are really nice."

Again, her smile, the look in her eyes, struck him as sincere.

"Yes indeed, who knows? I hope we do. Bump into one another."

He could hear that merry laugh of hers until the door of the club car hissed shut behind him. After the train had pulled away, waiting in the taxi queue, he thought of her. She was younger than him, he guessed, but not by much. Perhaps in her mid-forties. And very pretty, though not in any sort of glamorous way. Sort of a healthy Midwest way was the best he could describe it. They hadn't even exchanged names, yet the talk between them had been honest and unforced, as if they had known one another longer than the few minutes they did. How strange and full they could be, he thought. Those little moments in life that came and went so quickly.

***

The apartment was a second floor unit in a building on a street just across from the sea, with a bedroom just big enough to contain a double bed and a small table. One person could move comfortably in the kitchen because they did not have to move far. Standing in front of the sink everything, icebox, stove, microwave, and cabinets, was within an arm's reach.

Not even a Gideon's Bible for a lost soul such as him to find comfort in. Not that he had read the Bible recently. Not since he was a kid with his mother. And he wasn't a lost soul anymore. He had decided that in Madrid.

But the location of the apartment was a plus, as Emmitt discovered the next day, after a night of good sleep in the tiny bedroom. Refreshed, he took a cup of coffee and wandered out into the grounds stretching away from the two-building complex. The grass had been cut recently and in the slight breeze coming off the Mediterranean the smell of the freshly mown lawn carried just a hint of salt. The sea, itself, was visible across the wide boulevard running past the front of the complex. He could see the tall masts of yachts anchored off from the shore, their colored pennants wafting in the breeze as he sat with his coffee on a bench beneath an oak tree, surrounded by a circle of colorful flowers opening up in the morning light.

No, it wasn't as bleak as he had thought. Tired from the trains he had let the sparseness of the apartment get to him. But it was too lovely of a morning—the fresh cut grass, the colorful flowers seeming to blossom even more as he sat. The Med on the other side of the highway and traffic sounds from the road signaling that there were people, alive and going about their business already that day. Indeed, way too lovely a morning to waste.

He took the bus to Old Town. It was a pleasant ride down a tree-lined boulevard filled with both homes and shops, many with an Italian feel to their design. After getting off the bus at the stop in front of the Hotel de Ville, he crossed over the wide La Croissette to the harbor side and walked down toward the Film Festival hall.

The day was coming on fresh and clean now, the air dry and mild, with only little wisps of fluffy clouds hanging in an otherwise blue sky. The mountains off in the distance shimmered in a light blue haze the same color as the sky and the water below. The harbor itself was full of more boats than Emmitt had ever seen in one place before. Some of these were docked at the slips, while further out bigger yachts swung at anchor in the bay. Sailboats, motor boats, sport fishing craft, both simple and not, jet boats, and plain wooden commercial craft, bobbed in the wind and tide.

The scene was straight out of a travel book—tourists in colorful summer garb strolling along in front of the famous Film Hall, people old and young, couples or alone, smiling in the sunshine and apparently enjoying themselves very much. To his surprise, Emmitt was enjoying himself as well.

After realizing he had pretty much seen what there was to see, he crossed back over the boulevard to the shade of the shops and cafes on the other side. Standing on the corner, unsure of where he wanted to go, he glanced up the side street winding away behind him. A familiar red and white striped pole graced the door of a little shop—and Emmitt knew exactly what was right for that moment.

"Bonjour, m'siuer," the barber, said as Emmitt entered. He was busy trimming an older gentleman's wispy gray mustache and beard, the light click of the scissors resonating in the otherwise quiet little shop.

"Bonjour." Emmitt held two fingers to the side of his head, making cutting motions with them.

"Oui, oui." The barber, a young man in his late twenties or early thirties waved him to an empty chair. Next to the chair was a rack containing the day's *Le Monde* and *Le Figaro,* but no English papers. Below these were some French versions of the men's soft porn magazines that had graced barber shops for time immemorial. Emmitt picked one and sitting in the chair waiting his turn, flicked through the pages of topless lovelies smiling and looking very unreal.

When it was Emmitt's turn in the chair he found the barber to be very efficient, focusing his attention on the task at hand and limiting conversation to simple questions such as, "You like Cannes, m'siuer?" and, "Have you been to the beaches?" Here the barber tapped with his scissors the magazine Emmitt still held in his lap. "Pretty girls, oui?"

"Oui," Emmitt answered. "Beaucoup."

Looking in the mirror running the length of the wall behind the two chairs while he paid the man Emmitt noticed how the black in the salt and pepper aspects of his hair, was losing ground. Well, he was going to be 54 soon. *Not getting any younger*, he thought. With a "merci" and a wave he was out the door.

Out on the main drag he could feel the breeze coming from the harbor below. The wind carried a scent of salt, a pleasant relief from the stifling confines of the narrow side street. It was pushing noon and the cafes lining the sidewalk were beginning to fill with people. He hadn't thought of it until then, but he was getting hungry. He found a café and ate a dozen oysters on the half-shell, and some thick French crackers he didn't know if he liked or not. With them he drank a very cold dark German bock that he *did* like.

A good way to end a first morning in a town he was unsure of, he thought, as he headed toward the Hotel de Ville and the bus back to where he was staying. There was a hammock swung between two trees on the wide lawn in front of the apartment building. Emmitt had a vision of himself in that hammock, *Swann's Way* open on his chest as he dozed in the warm Mediterranean afternoon air.

But someone—a balding overweight man of indeterminate origin in a Speedo that Emmitt thought he had no business wearing—had beaten him to the hammock. With the hammock no longer an option, the beach would have to do.

In the one closet the apartment provided he found beach towels, and mats. With a bottle of water, a towel and mat under his arm, he set off. The beach was supposed to be only a five minute walk from the complex. At first he thought he might have missed it, because it didn't seem like much of a beach. But after walking a little further down the sidewalk—where there was no beach at all, only rocks—he figured he was wrong and turned back. This local spot was nothing like the white beaches glimmering in the morning sun he'd seen on the train there the day before. Instead, the sand was gray color, and he had to watch out for rocks buried beneath it when he left the sidewalk.

Other than Emmitt, the only people on the beach were a young couple with a child, a boy, perhaps four or five years old. It was quiet and peaceful, and Emmitt lay back on the mat with his eyes closed to the sun.

He couldn't get comfortable on the mat, though, and after a while sat up again, holding his knees against his chest. The water looked inviting—deep sparkling blue and promising a relieving coolness, graced by sailboats further out heading off to wherever. He found he had to walk out quite a ways, not only to escape the matted clusters of sea grass in the shallow water by the shore, but to find water deep enough he could actually swim in. Even then, if he put his feet down to stand in neck deep water, the sea grass was still there.

But he stuck with it, the water just cold enough to be refreshing but not a shock to the system. He swam for maybe a hundred yards, following the coast, and then back, and feeling good with what he had done, he made his way back to his towel and mat waiting on the shore.

Letting the sun dry him, he saw that a woman had joined the young couple down from him. This woman was a girl, really, like the mother, neither one of them possibly older than their mid-twenties. The difference, though, between these two women, being that the newcomer had taken her bikini top off. Her breasts were pale and shining in the mid-afternoon sunlight—like those of the girls in the men's magazine at the barber shop.

He didn't mean to stare. Didn't think that he was, really. Just at that moment the topless girl happened to look Emmitt's way. She paused, took a *long* look at him—and waved. The wave, and the smile that went with it, seemed friendly enough. But he turned away quickly to look out at the sea, wondering why he suddenly felt uncomfortable.

Damnit, that was how the old Emmitt would feel. He was leaving that man behind. The day was as perfect and fine as one could wish and he was in a better than fine place to enjoy it. When the girl looked his way again, this time it was *he* who waved—and smiled.

***

The next morning he made the mistake of taking the bus to Nice, an hour's drive, in very crowded conditions. As they drove up the coast, stopping at every little town along the way, the skies over the Med started to cloud up with big thunderheads moving in. Once in Nice, finally free of the confines of the bus and the chattering people, Emmitt felt better. He decided to take the train back, a move that would cut the travel time in half and probably be in less crowded quarters.

The rain held off long enough for him to walk the cobblestoned streets of the town center and get a feel of the place. He had lunch in a British pub by the harbor, where he ate a Shepard's pie and drank Guinness stout. Nice was okay, but he liked Cannes better. His lunch done, he walked back to the train station and boarded the next one back, just as the threatening skies opened up.

It continued to rain the next few days, stopping only, that first night, at least, so that he was able to walk down the street to a little Italian place he'd found. The food was very good and they served an excellent local red wine, both of which went a long ways toward cutting the edge off the rainy day. Other than that he stayed in the apartment, listening to the radio, reading Proust, and when the rain let up enough, dashing out to get a meal, or buy groceries.

On Friday morning the rains broke, the day coming on as clear and mild as anyone could wish for. There wasn't a cloud in the sky. The morning temperature might be just on the edge of being cool, but not so cool that one couldn't enjoy being in the water and Emmitt grabbed the bus for the public beach on the north end of Cannes.

The beach itself was speckled with people, their blankets, colorful towels and umbrellas and beach chairs spread out on the white sand. Like the girl at the beach a few days back who had smiled and waved at Emmitt, women were sunning topless. Some of them were of an age Emmitt felt might be better served by leaving their tops on. Not that it was any of his business, he thought as he walked down to the water and dove in, letting the coolness of it clear his brain, like the air bubbles slowly seeping from his lips as he swam underwater, letting it all go.

While he had been swimming and treading water he had been aware of children by the shore, splashing and playing on the edge of the water. But when he surfaced Emmitt saw how another child, a boy maybe five or six, was dog paddling along. Halfway between Emmitt and the shore, he was away from the other children and any nearby adult that Emmitt could see. Even Emmitt, no parent, could tell that the little boy was further out than he should be by himself.

Thinking that he must be wrong, Emmitt started to swim in. A rock jetty curved one end of the beach to make it into a cove; Emmitt wanted to take his book, sit on the rocks, and dry off in the sun. Then the little boy alone in the water went under.

Emmitt didn't think much of it at first. Figuring that the boy wanted to swim underwater a little bit, he continued his leisurely stroke toward shore. But when the little boy broke surface, even at a distance Emmitt could see that something wasn't right. The boy went under again. Suddenly Emmitt was swimming hard to where he had been just seconds before, wondering as he swam why no one else had seen what he had, and where the lifeguard was. Maybe the boy was just playing around. Some sort of solitary diving game in the water. But even if he didn't know anything about kids, the scared look on his face, his eyes wide, his arms, paddling fast against the water failing to keep him up, no, that didn't seem like any game.

Emmitt didn't know anything but the slicing of his arms through the water. Water that had seemed so buoyant and giving, until he was in a hurry with a purpose and a place to be. Now it felt as if he were swimming through glue. Felt as if he were swimming in a nightmare, unable to save someone, unable to save himself.

And then he was there. At the spot he could swear the child had been. And yet, nothing. Just a seabird of some kind wheeling in the clear sky overhead. He looked down into the water and yes, there *was* the boy. Underwater and sinking. And then Emmitt, too, was underwater, holding his breath, hoping it wasn't too late. He wasn't. The kid squirmed and kicked when Emmitt reached him, grabbed him, and began to swim upwards. Though it seemed like it took forever, the two of them broke the surface, Emmitt gasping for air and pulling hard for the shore.

He thought suddenly of his child as he swam, holding on tight to the boy. Of Emily—and how he hadn't ever been there for her. To offer the comforts of safety and security as a father should. And yet here he was, years after his own child's birth, for another child, one he didn't know and had only done for what his instincts screamed at him to do

They made it to the shallows. Holding the boy under one arm like a football, Emmitt came out of the water onto the beach. Suddenly adults *were* present and paying attention. Emmitt heard one voice loudly over the others, a woman, screaming, "Robbie. Oh my God! Robbie!"

It was the woman from the train.

"Robbie," the woman screamed again as she pushed her way through the people gathered around Emmitt and the boy. "Oh my God, Robbie, are you okay?" Without waiting for an answer she picked the boy up and held him tight in her arms. The blonde hair falling down to her shoulders was the same as it had been on the train. but the trilling laugh of delight were gone—replaced by a look of gut-wrenching fear. A look very familiar to Emmitt from having seen it on his own face. In the mirror in the hospital bathroom where he had gone to collect himself after hearing from the doctor the awful truth about Dana.

"He's okay," Emmitt said, uncomfortable with all the people around and the worry in the woman's face—as well as his sudden remembrance of that day in the hospital..

"I took my eyes off him for just a minute. This woman was asking me if I was American," she said, rocking the little boy in her arms. "She wondered if I could tell her how to get to the harbor where they have the famous festival," she continued, as if it made all perfect sense to this stranger who had just rescued her boy. "It was just a minute, I swear!"

"I got to him in plenty of time," Emmitt cut in. "I'm sure he's okay. Maybe a little scared. With good reason to be. I'm just glad I was close enough to help him."

Because there was no denying it. The kid could have died. He was sinking and not coming up. Not on his own at any rate. It was only when Emmitt had hold of him and was pulling for the surface that the boy started to kick his legs in order to help.

Only then. And if Emmitt hadn't been around, not in the water and close enough to help, he didn't want to think of what might have happened instead. A shudder ran through his body. No, he didn't want to think of that scenario at all.

He wanted to say something more reassuring to the woman, and the boy, who was smothered in her arms. But she didn't give him a chance. Holding the boy against her chest, she turned and hurried off down the beach, the crowd parting to let her through. Just like that, it was all over: the adrenaline rush gone. All of it over and as quickly as it had happened, and nothing left but the water, the beach, the bright sun overhead shining down through a clear sky, the people there to enjoy both the sun and the water, coming and going, unaware that just minutes before *something* out of the usual had gone down.

Retreating to his things, Emmitt gathered them up and made his own journey across the sand. As he was stepping into the elevator back at the apartment he wondered if he would see the woman again. Twice now in a short space of time they had crossed one another's path. He hoped there would be a third time. Suddenly he hoped that very much.

***

Funny, but over the next few days he couldn't stop thinking of the woman from the train and on the beach—wondering if he might run in to her again. The next morning, Saturday, he took the train up the coast, getting off in Antibes. There were places to go and sights to see and he might as well get to it. He spent the day walking the cobblestoned streets of Antibe's Old Town, down to the harbor and along the beach. It was only on the way back to Cannes that he remembered the woman had said she was staying in Antibes with her sister and brother-in-law. Yet, there had been no chance run in with her. Apparently, he decided as the train pulled into Cannes, the Fates had decreed otherwise.

Trying to put the woman out of his mind, on Monday he made a trip up to Monaco. It was a pleasant train ride along the coast, he spent the night in a little hotel off from the glitz and lights, lost a small amount of money in the casino, got half buzzed on wine, caught the train back in the morning, and crossed Monaco off his mental lists of places he should probably go to, seeing as how he was in the neighborhood. Tuesday he stopped in at the tourist information stand by the train station in Cannes to inquire about the local fishing. He was interested in doing some trout fishing up in the mountains beyond the coast, he told the girl behind the counter. She gave him some brochures, that when he looked at them that night weren't of much help. Wednesday he spent most of the day at the beach across from the Croisette where he had last seen the woman and saved the little boy. The day was warm, almost downright hot, and the water cold and refreshing. Thursday was cloudy, showers fell off and on, and he spent most of that day in the apartment listening to the radio, reading his copy of *Swann's Way*, and napping. Friday, came on clear and nice, and to stretch his legs he walked down to a boulangerie on the Croisette for breakfast.

As he came up to the little bakery he spotted a woman sitting at one of the outside tables. A woman with blonde hair, her head down, apparently reading a newspaper unfolded on the table in front of her. A woman, who when she looked up from the paper just then, happened to be the one he had been looking for.

"It's you," Emmitt blurted out, immediately embarrassed for doing so. But the woman smiled, or made an attempt to, through a face pale and drawn.

"Yes, it's me. Have you been looking for me."

"I haven't. Though I *have* been worried about you and the boy—after what happened on the beach and all." Caught up in his honesty, he added, "You guys vanished so fast I was left wondering if any of it really happened."

"Oh, it really happened. Believe me, it really did." She made no effort at smiling this time. "I wanted to get Robbie looked at as quickly as I could. When I called my sister and told her I was taking him to the clinic in town, she stopped me. Her husband's friend was a doctor and could be at the house by the time we got there. She wanted me to let him handle it. A matter of discretion I suppose, what with her husband's position and all."

"He looked okay when you left." Emmitt sat down at the little table across from her while the rest of the morning continued on around them, two strangers talking about something pertaining only to them. "Of course, I'm no doctor, so what do I know?"

"His lips were turning blue and he was coughing pretty hard by the time we got to the car. I didn't waste any time getting him back. I knew Jaguars were a fast car, just never thought I'd be driving one at a hundred along a road in France!"

"Wow!"

She must have noticed Emmitt was empty handed across the table from her, or perhaps she was embarrassed from talking so much, but she asked, "We're you coming here to begin with, or just passing by and stopped when you saw me?"

"Actually, my plan was to get coffee and a croissant."

"Go, then, please. Don't let me stop you."

Funny, but he didn't really want to leave, to go through the act of getting up, going into the bakery, ordering, paying, and didn't want to do any of that and leave the moment he was in.

"I'll be right back," he told her, instead. "Would you like more coffee?"

"You know, I would. I haven't been sleeping well at all lately. Not since the beach. I'm afraid caffeine is the only thing keeping me going these days."

"Caffeine it is, then."

It was close to noontime when she suddenly realized how long they had been talking and told Emmitt she had to go. By then they had properly introduced themselves, her name bring Jane Singleton. She was a widow. "A year now," she said, and when he told her he was sorry she waved him off, Emmitt wondering how easily she did so, wondering as well if she might tell him one day. She was spending the month of September, she continued, and part of October with her sister Carol, and her husband, in Antibes. "I believe I told you that on the train."

"Yes, you did."

"It was terrible what happened on the beach. With Robbie. Jesus, he could have died. You know?"

"But he didn't," Emmitt said, aware that suddenly, wherever the conversation might be headed now, pleasant banter between two tourists meeting for coffee was not going to be a part of it.

"Robbie is Carol's grandson," Jane continued, her blue eyes holding steady on Emmitt. "He's staying with her and his grandfather while his parents are on an UN mission in Russia. Carol wasn't feeling well that day and I offered to take Robbie to the beach. You know, give her some quiet time. I should have known better—about not taking my eyes off of him while he was in the water. I raised two kids of my own after all. But when that tourist lady stopped and asked if I was American, could I tell her how to get down to the harbor and the Film Institute. Well, things can happen so fast anymore. I happened to look up and see you coming out of the water with Robbie and I just lost it. I haven't been able to sleep since. He seems to have forgotten the whole thing but I certainly haven't. Have dreams about it almost every night. This is the first day since then that I've been out of the villa. I've felt so paralyzed, worse even than when my husband died. Carol, and Jared, too, have been really kind about the whole thing. But if they have forgiven me I just can't seem to forgive myself."

Emmitt let her talk, nodding his head here and there, adding only once that he was glad he had been there and could help.

"Thank God, you were there. It makes my skin crawl to think about what might have happened if you weren't. Carol, hell, my niece and Robert—Robbie's dad. How could I let them down like that? That's what I keep asking myself."

"Well, the good news is that no one was let down."

"I was," she interrupted, her eyes red from crying. "I let myself down."

"Yes, but again, it all came out all right."

Damned if she didn't break down completely then—while people walked by on the busy avenue, in and out of the bakery, and on to elsewhere. Emmitt didn't care—he only cared right then to do something to help her with her pain, the only thing he knew to do being to get up from the little table and walk around to her, pull her to her feet and hold her in his arms.

"I'd like to see you again," Emmitt said when her crying stopped, she realized the time, and said she had to go.

That would be nice, she told him. The weekend was out, though. Her sister had houseguests for the weekend; she wanted all of the family to be there to meet them.

"A count," Jane said. "And his wife, the Countess. From Luxemburg, I believe. Or one of those little principalities where everyone is insanely rich."

"It sounds interesting."

"You mean boring, don't you? The Count, I'm told, is very big with a start-up tech company. The weekend will mostly be business between him and Jared. But my presence has been requested, so I must be there."

She could get away Monday. Would he like to come to Antibes for lunch? He would, and the arrangements were made.

"Thank you very much, Emmitt," she said.

"For what?"

"For being there that day. And for being here today."

She turned and walked away down the Croissete before he could tell her, you're welcome.

***

On Monday morning Emmitt took the 9:45 train to Antibes. When it rolled into the station at 10:20 she was waiting for him on the platform. He couldn't remember a time in the recent past when the sight of another human being—one there for the express purpose of meeting him—had gladdened him as much as the fact of this woman, Jane Singleton, did right then.

Like in a movie. The way she came out into the pale light of the overhead fluorescents, crushing out a cigarette with one sandaled foot on the concrete platform as she did so. He tried to think of the last time he had been with a woman who smoked and came up with Jeri, his college girlfriend—this followed by the sobering thought, *You've not been with this woman.*

As politely as he could. Emmitt pushed through the others to get off the train and onto the platform where she seemed to have disappeared. Suddenly, there she was again, right in front of him, all blonde and blue-eyed and smiling as she took his hand and turned to lead him out of the station. He hesitated, wanting badly to take her in his arms, even if he knew it was much too early to do such a thing. Perhaps she sensed this, but if she did it didn't seem to bother her. If anything her smile grew even brighter.

"Come along, Emmitt" she said. "The car's this way."

Out of the station, Emmitt felt he should say something. Not sure exactly what, he managed, "I didn't know you smoked."

"Oh, you saw me." She still had him by the hand, something he liked very much. "My dirty little secret."

"As *dirty secrets* go it's not too bad. I used to. Camels. A man's cigarette, I told myself." He shrugged. "Now there's a cigar every once in a while."

"I really don't smoke that much," she said. "Maybe four or five a day, with wine or a cocktail. When I'm nervous."

He was going to let the "nervous" thing pass, then didn't. "You were nervous just now? Waiting for me?"

"Yes." It was so blatantly honest, which he liked just as much as her hand holding his. "Weren't you? Nervous about this, even just a little?"

He felt bad for a moment; her face had gone so serious, then admitted, "I *was* very nervous."

And there it was, the laugh of hers he remembered from the train.

"Here we are." She dug in the purse slung over her shoulder for the keys. "Are you hungry, or would you like to see some of the town first?"

"Let's do that," he said. The car, black and shiny in the sunlight, was a late-model Jaguar sedan. He ran a finger along the edge of the hood, touched the gunmetal gray Jaguar hood ornament. "I see you drive in style."

"The car's my sister's, sad to say."

He couldn't decide if there was a note of apology in her tone, or not. If so, it didn't suit her.

"Like the villa every year, she rents one of these for the season."

She looked at him then with those startling blue eyes and he realized he was correct. There was no apology in her for anything at all.

"My sister married well, as they say." Jane went to open the door to the driver's side of the Jag but Emmitt beat her to it, holding it for her as she slid in behind the wheel. "She's happy and I'm glad for her. But come along now," she said, as she had earlier in the station. "Let me show you around beautiful little Antibes."

They drove down to the old port. With an hour to go until noon what was left of the morning remained clear and mild, the smell of the nearby sea drifting through the open windows of the Jag. Jane was wearing a colorful sun dress with cut-off sleeves, the color of which almost matched the color of the sea when the afternoon sun on the Riviera shone upon it. A little silver cross dangling on a frail silver chain, hung just above the V-neck of the dress, standing out against the red of her skin from her days in the sun since the train.

He also noticed how her feet—in some sort of silver sandals that matched the chain around her neck—expertly worked the gas, clutch, and brake pedal as she wheeled the Jaguar through the narrow streets of the town. She was a good driver, comfortable with the five-speed, down-shifting into the turns instead of relying solely on the brake, and her comfortableness behind the wheel was relaxing.

"You approve?" They were at a stop light, a line of tourists crossing the street in front of them. "Or disapprove?"

"Excuse me?"

"My driving. You seemed awfully intent on what I was doing."

Christ, I can be such a fool.

"Oh. Yes, I approve. Very much." And to add even more to his embarrassment, said "You're a good driver."

Not only a fool, but a stupid one at that.

"I'm glad." The light changed and they eased off, up ahead of them at the end of the narrow street, the port opening up and the high ramparts protecting it, gray and silent in the noon sunlight coming on. "I like to drive. The summer after my junior year in college my dad bought me a new Camaro. A present for my good grades, he said. A wonderful present it was, too! I spent the months before school started in the fall driving across the country, from San Francisco to New York. By myself. Stopping where I wanted, when I wanted, just taking my time. It was so freeing. When I came back for my senior year I couldn't stop thinking about where I'd go next, when summer came. Mexico crossed my mind a lot. Thought I might just drive all the way down to South America. I met my husband, though, that year. Got married, never did go to Mexico, and the rest, as they like to say, is history."

A casual reminder, out in the open between them now as she pulled into the parking lot, that she had a past. Some of which she had just revealed—more of it that she had not. It was good, Emmitt felt, that they had pulled in and parked the car at that moment, and he didn't have to say anything. Lest his own past and attendant sorrows come out and shadow what could very well be a good day.

The stone ramparts Emmitt had noticed at the stoplight, protected a cove full of boats of various sizes. The arc created by the stone work opened up into a bigger bay. Beyond this bay, the Mediterranean. People strolled along the top of the high walls. The stone ramparts, the sea lying beyond those walls, reminded him of the old fort at St. Augustine back in Florida—of a weekend trip his mother had taken him on to that city when he was child of maybe seven or eight. To see our country's very first city, she had told him. So you can learn something about where we all came from. Emmitt hadn't thought about that trip— or his mother—in a long time. Now it all came flooding back to him and he turned to Jane, busy straightening her hair and putting on sunglasses after locking up the car.

"Can we go up there?" he said, pointing to the steps leading up to the top of the walls. "Before we go into town?"

"Sure." She smiled at him. A little quizzically, he thought. "The view from there is fantastic."

It was, too. At the bend where the walls opened toward the sea, he could see to the north the lighthouse on the very tip of Cap D'Antibes. Below and beyond, the water, shimmering blue all the way to the horizon. Out of nowhere he wondered if his daughter, a grown woman by now and on her own most likely, had ever been to places like this — places where the world opened all the way up for one to see, feel, and enjoy.

Thinking of this, as well as of that trip with his mother, he asked Jane — still holding his hand as she had at the train station, which felt surprisingly natural — if she ever brought the boy up here.

"Oh yes," she laughed. "Other than the beach, it's his favorite place here. He likes to pretend he's a soldier, or better yet, a pirate, when we're up here. From the old days, he says. My grand-nephew has quite the imagination," and she laughed again.

"Good for him."

Emmitt's mother had said much the same thing about him. When he was a boy — around the same age as Robbie — and eager to tell her a story of some kind he had made up, stories in which he was always the hero, and his mother the one he had to save from whatever danger his young mind could imagine.

"An imagination can help in this crazy world of ours."

"You think?" And again, that quizzical little smile.

"It helped me," he said, then looked out again at the sea, not ready yet to go into detail how "imagination" had helped him in his life.

"Maybe you and I could bring Robbie up here sometime," Jane said in an offhand way. "On another trip?"

Without missing a beat Emmitt told her, "Yes, I'd like that." It was true. He would like that very much. "How is he doing, by the way?"

"He's doing great, back to his old self."

"And you?"

"Getting there, more so every day. Thanks for asking. That's sweet of you."

It was hot up on top of the ramparts, with nothing to block or deflect the sunlight, and only the slight breeze off the sea to cool the air. Noticing beads of sweat on Jane's forehead, Emmitt suggested they go into the town. She readily agreed. Once past the stone archway over the entrance to Old Town they walked along a narrow street where the buildings on both side provided a little shade from the sun. Soon the street opened up into a market where brightly colored tarps and canvas awnings protected the stalls displaying spices, jellies, wines, cured meats, and more. A quartet of formally dressed musicians had gathered on one corner, playing for coins from passers-by. According to Jane, this went on every day.

"Except Sunday," she added.

"Church?" Emmitt asked as he tossed a euro into the hat.

"Yes. The French are very religious, you know."

"Even with all the wine and lovemaking they go in for?"

"Yes! Probably why so many of them make it a point to be in church come Sunday."

"How about you?" With that quizzical little grin back on her face, Emmitt quickly added, "Church, I mean. Not the wine and the lovemaking."

She leaned against him and said, "Sad to say I've been a stranger to both church and the other two you mentioned."

"That *is* sad." He had let go of her hand when he dropped the euro into the musician's cup, but reached for it again as they walked on. "Me, too. Likewise guilty. On two counts, anyway. Church and lovemaking. Fortunately wine has not been absent from my life."

He could see his face reflected back at him in the big oval sunglasses she wore, wondering when the last time had been that he smiled as big and wide as the one he saw in the dark lenses covering her eyes. Apparently he was enjoying himself.

"As a matter of fact, I hope to enjoy a glass or two at lunch."

They were both laughing as she led him through another of those stone archways and to the steps of an old building.

"Do you like Picasso?"

"Not as much as the Impressionists, but he's definitely interesting," Emmitt said. "I saw some of his work in Madrid. The one from the Spanish Civil War, *Guernica*, I liked very much "

"Well then, lucky for us, Antibes has a very nice Picasso museum. Right here at the top of the steps."

"Let's go," he said.

But according to the sign posted on the heavy wooden doors at the top of the steps, the museum was closed on Mondays.

"Damn it all," he said. "At least it gives me a reason to come back another day. One of several reasons, actually."

"Oh? And what might those other reasons be?" she teased.

A wind came up from the water and blew her blonde hair back from her forehead. Though her eyes were not visible behind the sunglasses, Emmitt could imagine how they looked as she smiled and tugged at her wayward hair.

"I think you know."

"Really?"

Her laugh drifted out over the sea like the seabirds wheeling here and there over the water.

He was getting hungry. From the walking, yes and from the woman, too. There was no denying that. Suddenly he was hungry for everything.

"Ready for lunch, Emmitt?" Her simple question was a jolt thrown into his already running consciousness. "We've been walking for quite a while. I don't know about you, but I'm about starved."

"You're reading my mind." And quickly added, "Jane." Saying her name aloud like that felt almost as good as hearing her say his his. "You decide. You know the town better than I do. After all, I'm just a visitor."

"Technically I'm a visitor, too. Even though I've been coming here for ten years now. But I'm glad you're leaving lunch to me. I know just the place." With a shy smile she said, "You're a very welcome visitor, by the way. Just thought I'd let you know."

They headed back toward town, walking awhile before they turned into a side street. The street was cobblestoned like many of the others in the town, the buildings here rising up on both sides so close they could almost touch one another at the top across the street. In another moment, though, Jane led him through an open doorway, and up a narrow flight of circular stairs. Six stories up, the stairs opened onto a wide terrace where, beneath a bright red and white striped awning, hanging plants and potted palm trees surrounded a cluster of small tables. Beyond the people and the tables, over the rooftops of Antibes ,Emmitt could see the Med, all blue and sparkling in the afternoon sun.

Just like that, the close confines of the narrow street below, the whole town of Antibes, were left behind, the two of them, Emmitt and Jane, sitting at one of the little tables, covered with a checkered table cloth the same color as the awning overhead, the sea and the cloudless sky stretching out away from them to enjoy.

"Wow."

"Yes, my feelings exactly," Jane said. "The first time my sister brought me here."

"I didn't see a sign. Does this place have a name?"

"I don't know. That's what I asked my sister and she told me the same thing. I was about to ask the waiter, but Carol stopped me before I could, told me that might be tacky. I had to agree with her when I thought about it."

"Nothing wrong with a little mystery, yes?"

"I think so."

Over lunch—a filet of sole for Emmitt, very light and good in a white sauce, quiche Lorraine for Jane who told him it was what she always ordered there—they talked. He told her a little about his time in Paris, Madrid, and the rest of it. Paris was a great city, he said, there was so much to see and do in that town. "Wasn't that the truth," Jane said, adding that Paris was probably her favorite city in the world. Madrid was impressive, he added, but he had picked the wrong time of year for Pamplona. He might go back for the festival sometime. Just to say he'd done it. He wasn't sure. It probably wasn't that important to him. She had been to a bullfight once, in Madrid, actually, with her husband. She still didn't know if she had liked it or been appalled. That was five years ago. "You'd think I would know by now. My husband enjoyed it, had always wanted to see one, so I was glad for his sake." Emmitt started to say something, but she cut him off.

"You're not married, Emmitt?"

"I was. She passed away. Almost three years ago."

It was the first time that saying it out loud like that did not wrench all the way through to his gut—when he looked up from his food there was that lovely smile of hers across the table from him.

"How strange," Jane said. "Us both being widows. Well, actually, you're a widower." And then adding, her face a little flushed with embarrassment, "I'm sorry for your loss, Emmitt."

"Thank you."

"I want to miss him. I really do. But sometimes it's hard to do. And I feel guilty saying that."

She continued on before he had to make some sort of reply.

"But Ray drank. Turned mean when he did. I put up with it for a long time. For the sake of our children, you know."

Of course, Emmitt didn't know, not at all, and was saved again when she didn't give him the chance to say that he did.

"He fell for another woman. A younger one, of course. We were in the middle of the divorce when he died. Heart attack brought on by years of his alcoholism. His death ended the need for a divorce, of course. Ended his plans to marry the girl, too. Poor woman ended up with nothing."

"That's good. Right?"

"Yes. But sad, too, in a way."

She paused and then asked, "Do you miss your wife?"

"Yes." He did not want to go into how much, though, and was surprised when he said, "Not as much as I used to."

"I'm glad you're getting through it, Emmitt."

"So am I."

Two men carrying violins wandered into the little café. Instead of sending them away the maître d' allowed them to set up in a corner of the open terrace. Emmitt recognized them as being part of the quartet that had been playing in the street earlier. The lilting tones of the tunes they began to play brought an end to the dark mood threatening to engulf the lunch with Jane.

When lunch was over Jane had to get back. A phone call she had to make to the States to her attorney. Lingering details over her husband's will not yet resolved.

Walking back through town to the car it appeared that everything needed to be said between them, had been. Instead they were quiet, just walking, her hand again in his, all the good of the morning, and the lunch there with them.

It was only awkward at the train station when she dropped him off in front of the building.

"I really don't mean to just rush off like this," Jane said and he could see that she meant it in her eyes. "But I do have to go."

"That's perfectly okay." He could feel the hum of the engine idling in his thighs as he sat next to her in the car. "You don't want to disappoint lawyers."

"No, I guess not." And then, and serious, "I don't want to disappoint you, either."

"You haven't. Not at all." It was quiet for a moment, Emmitt not quite ready to leave, Jane apparently feeling the same. "I'd like to see you again. Maybe for dinner? I could show you around my town. Cannes."

"I'd like that. Very much."

That night, as he lay in bed reading *Swann's Way,* instead of focusing on the words on the page, he thought about the day with Jane. How it all went so easy between them, the stroll through town, the lunch at the strange little café with no name, and even the moments of awkwardness between them. The questions about one another's past were hard. But the strolling musicians who came into the café changed all that. And then the way she kissed him goodbye at the train station, just a light kiss, but not on his cheek as he expected, but on his lips, and though it wasn't passionate like the first time Sylvie had kissed him in Paris, there was a promise in Jane's lips on his, a promise that stayed with him on the train ride back to Cannes.

***

She met him for dinner Wednesday night at the Hotel Martinez on the Croissette. For a five star hotel Emmitt thought the food was a little disappointing. Jane agreed, though she said the after dinner brandy made up for it.

If the dinner, food wise, was a disappointment Emmitt felt that, brandy aside, *she* made up for it. The black evening dress she wore, laced with sequins that shimmered in the light of the chandeliers overhead, highlighted her hair and eyes. As far as Emmitt was concerned, he could have been eating a stale hamburger in a greasy dive in the heart of Miami and if she were there with him, dressed like that—not only the dress but just her and her smile across the table from him—he would not have minded.

After dinner they walked along the beach side of the Croissette, arm in arm. Because of the lights of the city behind them few stars were visible in the night sky. It was a shame, Emmitt thought. They would have to make do with the mast lights of the boats anchored in the bay winking on and off. Like at the train station he had that feeling of being in a movie—one of those films where two Americans, through a strange twist of circumstance, find themselves thrown together in a foreign land.

This was no movie, though, but real—real enough that while waiting on the light at a crosswalk he turned to her and said, "Let's go to my place."

Her voice was low and throaty, that quizzical little grin on her lips as she said, "Yes."

They were silent in the car on the ride over, silent as they walked across the parking lot of the apartment building and into the foyer. Silent while waiting for the elevator. Once the doors closed, though, and the elevator began its slow ascent to the third floor, he pulled Jane into his arms and kissed her. When the elevator stopped at his floor and they pulled apart, he said the first words either of them had spoken since the Croissette.

"I've been wanting to do that all day."

"Me, too."

The small, bare bones apartment seemed even smaller with her there. To cover his embarrassment at the lack of décor and the smallness of the place, as well as his sudden nervousness over what they were about to do, he offered her something to drink.

"No," Jane said softly, and was in his arms again, the apartment, the smallness of the living room, no longer a problem, his nervousness no longer an embarrassment, the night, her, him, all of it just the way it should be, and Emmitt aware—for once—that offers of a drink, small talk, any talking at all, were simply not necessary.

The first time they made love was quick, passionate, and hungry. Any worries he'd had about being with a woman after such a long time were gone. He came quicker than he wanted, aware she felt him do so, even through the condom—aware as well how glad he was he had gone into the little pharmacy down the street that morning and bought the condoms. Just in case, he'd told himself. Just in case.

He hated the thought that she would be disappointed. Instead she clutched him tighter, moving with her hips while using her hands on his naked buttocks in a way that seemed to say it was all right. It took him a minute or two before he realized that, surprisingly, he was still hard. Then they were making love again, none of the passion or hunger lost, but instead stretched out in a way he had never known before, until they both came—this time together.

Afterwards they lay on the bed side by side, faces turned to the ceiling, the light from a streetlamp across from the building seeped through the window to make an easy glow in the little bedroom. Emmitt was intensely aware of her next to him and her hurried breathing as it slowly relaxed.

How funny, he thought. He had known this woman for less than a week. Didn't really know her, really. Yet here she was. Here he was. If what happened between them was just a momentary fling in another country, the two of them lonely, and ready, and wanting to rid themselves of that loneliness and need, if only for a little while, then that was okay. But when she turned over on her side, atop of him actually, her face, so close to his, shining with just a little sheen of sweat, her eyes glistening, he didn't believe that would be the case. Didn't see how it could be.

With her lips against his, she said, "My, my, my."

To which Emmitt could only reply, "Yes indeed."

Her laughter filled all the other space around him.

The fact something wasn't the same is what woke him. Day was just breaking outside the building and the bedroom, no longer lit by the streetlamp, was now filled with the dull gray of the coming morning. That wasn't what woke him—it was that he was alone.

In the grogginess of being barely awake, his first thought was that she had never been there in the first place. That the whole evening had been a dream. Even half-awake as he was, Emmitt knew he couldn't have dreamt such a thing. It had been too vivid, too real. Rolling out of bed, he grabbed the pants he had left on the floor the night before and went looking for a clue as to where she had gone and why.

The search didn't take long. A sheet of memo paper propped up against the coffee maker in the tiny kitchen held the answer. *Dear Emmitt,* she had written. *Sorry to leave like this but you looked so peaceful sleeping I couldn't bring myself to wake you. Please forgive me! I did kiss you goodbye.*

In a simple, but graceful cursive that reading did something very pleasant to him, she had signed the note, *Jane.* She followed her signature with a PS, and—as if he could have forgotten—her phone number.

He smiled, his smile growing even wider as he began to make his morning coffee.

***

After that night and without either of them saying anything, Emmitt and Jane fell into an easy routine of spending their days together. She came down to Cannes or Emmitt took the train to Antibes, where she would meet him at the station as she had on that first day. Even though it was almost October the days were still warm and mild so a lot of their time together was spent on the beach.

Over this time Emmitt learned a lot about her—how she was a native born Californian. From Bodega where her father was in lumber business. How grateful she was to return home when her marriage split up, tired of the twenty years in LA with Ray and his car businesses, all of it so different from the serenity of the redwood forests north of San Francisco where she had grown up. How she met Ray when she was fresh out of Berkeley and a friend thought he would be a good date for Jane. He was charming, had money and though he was a little older he treated her nice, and enjoyed going to concerts of all kinds, rock, opera, and jazz. She thought he was handsome and a good lover and though her father was appalled when she told him they were getting married, said, "You're marrying a car salesman?" If her mother had been around Jane might have heard a different opinion. But she wasn't, dead of cancer over five years. But when the marriage ended her dad didn't gloat but told her over the phone, come on home, and she did.

As for Emmitt he told her some about himself, his writing work, his life with Dana and her illness, and how he was afterwards—told her as best he could, which he didn't think was very well.

Robbie accompanied them on these outings more often than not, and Emmitt found he didn't mind. Found in fact, that he enjoyed the little boy's company. The three of them swam, took long walks on the beach, the rock jetties, and for lunch went to one of the many cafes available on the shore side of the Croissette or in Antibes. Sometimes, at Robbie's insistence, instead of eating at a café their lunch consisted of hot dogs or baguettes from one of the stands scattered along the sidewalk fronting the beach. Taking this simple fare back to their blankets and chairs they picnicked by the water. Robbie said these were the best lunches and Emmitt discovered he felt that way, too.

The best part of this routine, for Emmitt, came about the very first time they spent the day like this—when by mid-afternoon it became apparent the little boy was getting tired, and according to his aunt, ready for a nap.

"I better take him home," Jane said.

Emmitt was disappointed with the day ending so early but said nothing. After gathering up their things and once back at the car, Jane told Robbie to thank Mr. Raines for the good time. Just before getting into the driver's seat of the Jag she whispered in Emmitt's ear.

"I'll come back after I drop him off." Her voice, her breath, so close to him like that was strangely exciting. "Okay?"

"More than okay."

Even with her promise to return he wasn't sure she would. He didn't know much about kids, other than idle talk at social gatherings from people who had them. From this casual talk, Emmitt gathered that children had the potential to change whatever plans their parents—or in this case, aunt—might have.

But an hour, maybe a little more, later, just as he was nodding off on the futon in the living room, he heard a soft knocking at the door. He opened it to find Jane standing in the hallway, wearing one of those colorful sundresses she seemed to favor, and holding a bottle of wine.

"The wine is for later," she said as she pushed past him into the apartment. "Right now I want you." She pulled him down on to the futon, all kisses and soft hands on his face and neck.

"I'm bad, aren't I?" Her voice was low and husky in his ear as it had been that first night they made love. She was busy pushing down the bathing suit he still had on. He was hard—had been from the moment he opened the door—and ready. When he was naked and her sundress up around her thighs and stomach, she guided him inside her. "Aren't I?" she repeated.

"Very bad," he told her and then couldn't say anything more.

Afterwards they sat on the futon, still naked, with the wine, no glasses, just passing the bottle back and forth, the slightly chilled redness of the wine refreshing and much needed. The last light of the afternoon in the apartment seemed to make her nipples, from where he had kissed and bitten them, look red and glistening like the wine they shared. He couldn't get over the richness of her body, the pale healthiness of her skin, the way she was soft and voluptuous, her breasts not overly big but just right as far as he was concerned. He had to marvel at the way she gave herself so totally, with a hunger he hoped he returned.

"So Mr. Emmitt Raines," she said, breaking the lovely silence he had lost himself in. "Call me curious—which I am by the way—but how do I compare?"

"Excuse me?"

"With the others."

"Oh, that."

There wasn't much to tell. Or at least he didn't think so. But he told her anyway—told her of the four women he had been with in his life, the last one his wife of over twenty years. Told her of the girl, Jeri, in college, who he supposed he had been in love with at the time, but he was young and she was his first girlfriend, so from the vantage point of all the time that had passed since then, well, he wasn't sure. He told her about Eileen and her sister Anna, and of the ugliness that occurred between them, and of how years later he learned about the daughter he'd had with Anna. And of how he had met and fallen for Dana and of how happy his life had been all the way up to the time she took sick and then died. When he was finished, he wondered how he felt about all of it—the telling of his past—and was happy it didn't take him long, sitting there with Jane naked on the futon drinking the wine, to realize that how he felt was better. Much better.

"Wow," is what Jane said when he was done, and then taking a deep breath, told him of her romantic partners over the years. This consisted of only two. The first one being a bumbling romance in college where she and the boy quickly discovered that they were each other's *first*, and probably because of that and their inexperience the sex was nothing what they thought it might be—at least not for Jane. She couldn't say how the boy felt because he never told her. But she was glad when he quit calling, and when it was over she didn't seek another. Then Ray Singleton came along, the next thing she knew they were married and having "legal" sex, as she put it.

"Ray certainly knew things I didn't," she told Emmitt.

Their sex life was a good one. Until his drinking became more important. He didn't seem to want her anymore, and when he did, usually when he was very drunk, was not able to perform.

"Now you understand why I am such a wanton lady," she finished with. "In my wild and wooly middle age. What do you think about that kind sir?"

"I'll show you what I think," he said.

They made love again, the afternoon finally gone, the bare apartment quiet and dark in the twilight.

Not every day went the same. Sometimes they met for a late dinner, after her sister and brother-in-law's guest were gone, a nightly occurrence at the villa because of his business. If they ended up back at his apartment and she spent the night, like the first time she did, Jane made sure she left early enough in the morning.

"For my sister," she told him when she left like that the first time. "Her husband is so prim and proper, and she feels when I'm staying with them, I should be, too. Seems silly in this day and age."

Emmitt wished she didn't have to leave like that, would have enjoyed sleeping in with her. He thought how be nice it would be to wake up in the morning, perhaps lazily make love, and then, after cleaning up and dressed, go down to the boulangerie by the bus stop for coffee and croissants. He could show her off to the matronly lady behind the counter, who with her thick dark hair piled atop her head and a very attractive smile, always greeted Emmitt when he came in with a, "Bonjour monsieur."

It was a lovely fantasy he thought more than once after Jane had left and he got out of bed, alone, and went down to the boulangerie. Not to be under current conditions, though. And this a thought that brought him up short once, just as he was to cross the street over to the bakery. What other conditions could there be?

Unable to—*maybe not wanting to*—consider the possibilities of other conditions, he continued on to the bakery, content for the time being with the friendly greeting from the matronly lady and the hot coffee and fresh croissant.

There was an afternoon that was a little different. "I have a confession to make," Jane said as they lay naked together on his bed.

"Will I have to absolve you of any sin you might have committed?"

"If I was Catholic and you were a priest and I were to tell you of my sinful thoughts, then yes. I suppose some Hail Mary's and some rosaries would be in order. But I'm not."

"That's good," Emmitt said. "I'm not feeling exactly priestly at the moment."

She looked so damned beautiful, he thought. The quizzical little grin was gone, in its place one of what he could only call complete surrender and contentment. He was happy to be a part of that smile.

"Don't keep me waiting," he said. "My curiosity knows no bounds."

"That afternoon on the train? Remember?"

"Very well."

"I wondered what you'd be like. You know? In bed."

"And?"

"I think you know." She laughed. "But what about you, Emmitt?" She sat up in the bed then, and in a rare display of modesty pulled the sheet up around her breasts.

"What about me?"

"Did you wonder what I might be like?"

"A priestly man such as myself? The thought never crossed my mind."

The whole exchange was such an honest admission between them — even if he hesitated for a moment before telling her that actually he *had* wondered about her a little. About her breasts. What they might look like. Might feel like. His admission seemed to answer her question, what with the way she slid back down in the bed and put her head up against his shoulder. All good stuff, he thought. The two of them together and happy with the time and the place and this falling in love thing. And again, like that morning on his way to the bakery, Emmitt was brought up short.

Fortunately, before he could go much further with his thoughts, Jane interrupted.

"Well?"

"Well what?"

"My breasts, as you call them. Do they meet to your satisfaction?"

"Oh, I guess so. They're all right."

"That's terrible!" The sheet dropped from her as she punched him lightly in the shoulder.

This time his laughter joined hers in filling the space all around him in the little bedroom.

***

The weather stayed warmed and pleasant enough for the beach and swimming all through the last week of September. Emmitt found himself teaching the boy how to swim, as opposed to the dog paddling he'd been struggling with when Emmitt came to his rescue. It wasn't planned, but one afternoon Emmitt — tired of watching the boy fooling around in the water with the water wings his aunt insisted he now wear, said it was time he learned how to really swim. Before going any further on this suggestion, and wondering if he might not be overstepping his bounds, he asked Jane what she thought about it.

"I'm damn near a stranger after all," he added. "Only met his parents that one time. Something like that should be their responsibility."

They were sitting on the sand up from the water where the boy was splashing around in the shallows, Jane's hair and eyes reflecting the sun streaming down on her, the sand, and the water, and forgetting his question for a moment, Emmitt wondering at the good fortune of late that had brought him to this place.

"His mom and dad are so busy all the time," Jane said. "Between this UN mission and the NGO Robert is to lead in Somali when they get back. Carol and John are taking him back with them to San Diego when they go. Putting him in school there until his parents are settled." She turned to him then and smiled, putting her hand on his shoulder. "My point being, in a roundabout way, is—though it might not be my decision to make—I think it is wonderful you take such an interest in Robbie. Are willing to teach him. I don't think his folks would mind at all. You certainly impressed them quite a bit the night we had dinner together at the 'mystery restaurant'. I will bring it up to them tonight and see what they think."

"I'm glad," Emmitt said, "that I made such a good impression on them. They seem like nice people. I'm glad, too, you trust me enough to let me show the boy how."

"Of course, I do!"

He didn't see Jane that night—her sister had invited just her out to dinner for some sibling bonding, according to Jane—and Emmitt spent a quiet evening at the apartment reading. Drifting off to sleep and thinking about the next day when he would try to teach Robbie how to swim, he thought of his own child. His daughter. Emily. His and Anna Hobart's child who he had had never known existed until she was four years old and the letter from Eileen Hobart came. He had dragged his heels about meeting her back then. Until so much time had passed he was too embarrassed by his actions to make the attempt. This certainly wasn't to his credit and he had known it even then. And done his best to shrug it off, to ignore it. To his loss, too, he was thinking now, as outside his open window he could hear the sounds of cars on the boulevard in the evening and the light wind from the Mediterranean brushing the limbs of the taller trees against the building. Very certainly to his loss.

As they had for the last two weeks, the morning came up bright and sunny, and as arranged, he met Jane and Robbie on the beach in front of the Hotel Martinez. It was fine, Jane told him, with Carol and her husband that Emmitt teach Robbie how to swim and they wanted him to know they were grateful for him doing so. Jane's only objection came when Emmitt had the boy leave the water wings on the shore.

"He's not a baby, Jane." He turned to the boy waiting eagerly at the water's edge. "You're not a baby are you, Robbie?"

"No." And to make sure his aunt heard him: "I'm no baby!"

"Now you're talking," Emmitt said. "We'll be fine, Jane. I promise. Remember? You said you trusted me."

"Okay, okay!"

Taking the boy's hand Emmitt led him out to where the water came up to his knees and the boy's chest. Crouching down he held him in his outstretched hands and began to instruct him in the proper way to do the Australian crawl. Robbie picked up the rudiments of the stroke pretty quickly. Emmitt couldn't help but laugh, though, at how he resisted leaving his face down in the water. Instead he kept it up while he swam.

Not exactly correct, Emmitt decided. But it was a good start and the boy's method seemed to work fine for him. By the end of the day they were swimming together along the shore in water just deep enough to do so. The boy—his blonde hair, slick and wet atop his head, and nearly invisible in the afternoon sun—seemed very proud of his achievement, judging by his laughter and the smile on his face.

The next day, a Saturday, Emmitt took the train to Antibes. It was the first of October and yet the sky was clear as a bell. The day looked to be much like the others preceding it, warm and mild with no hint of fall. Soon winter would blow down off the mountains, leaving the Riviera devoid of tourists. Fit only for the people who lived there year round. Emmitt had no idea how long the good weather would hold, but he hoped it would for a while longer. He was enjoying his time there too much to see it end. Even if he knew, that like the pleasant weather, his stay in Cannes and being with Jane—the boy as well—had to come to a close.

Just not anytime real soon, he thought as the train pulled into the now very familiar station where Jane and her nephew were waiting for him.

Being a Saturday the beaches were more crowded than during the week, people, chairs, blankets, and colorful umbrellas spread out along the sand as far as one could see. They found a spot for their stuff by the jetty jutting out into the water at the north end of the beach. The rocks made for a nice sheltered cove, just right for swimming. People, adults and children alike, were already in the water. After helping Jane with their things—towels, a big blanket to sit on, and the cooler packed with cold water, soft drinks for Robbie, and wine that Jane said was, "For later," Emmitt and the boy ran across the sand and into the easy surf, the water cool and cleansing for Emmitt after the crowded ride on the stuffy train.

A group of kids, boys and girls ranging in age from perhaps seven or eight—Robbie's age—up into their teens, were hanging out on the jetty. Some of the braver boys were jumping from the rocks into the water below. Emmitt noticed how Robbie couldn't seem to keep his eyes off the kids.

"I bet you'd like to try that, huh?"

"Yes!" Robbie was silent for a moment. "Aunt Jane won't let me."

"She might," Emmitt said. "If we ask her nice enough."

But Jane was more than hesitant about the idea. "I don't think so, Emmitt. Robbie's too young."

"He's no younger than that kid."

Emmitt pointed to a boy up on the rocks, his skin burned brown from a summer on the beach, who stood poised for a moment, maybe three or four feet above the water, and then jumped feet first.

"Yeah Aunt Jane," Robbie pleaded as the boy popped up to the surface to wipe the water from his eyes before swimming back to the rocks. "He's no older than me and he did it."

"It's not safe, Robbie," Jane said. "I'm just not comfortable about it at all."

"Nothing's safe in this world, Jane." The look she gave him was more than enough for Emmitt to realize it wasn't what she wanted to hear right then. Scrambling to recover he backtracked. "No, you're right." He hugged her there on the beach, her skin hot from the sun against his still wet from the water. "If you're uncomfortable with it, then we won't do it. Plain and simple."

"Thank you."

"Nothing to thank me for. I damn sure don't ever want to do something to make you uncomfortable. Not if I can help it. And this I can help." Turning to the boy he grabbed Robbie's hand. "Sorry kid. Your aunt says no, and that's all there is to it. Come on. I'll race you to the water. Last one in is a rotten egg."

The race down to the water was fun, Emmitt, of course, let Robbie beat him, and emboldened by his success, Robbie challenged him to a swimming race. As he had on the race down to the water, Emmitt let the boy beat him in the water. The look on Robbie's face, hair wet and hanging on his forehead, his eyes lit up with his success as Emmitt came up to the arbitrary finish line they had established, took Emmitt away.

Suddenly, his head filled with images of when he was a boy Robbie's age and learning how to swim. Long ago sunny days at the yacht club in Fort Lauderdale with his mother and his grandparents, John and Sadie Raines. The deference accorded the Raines family—John Raines, after all, being the man who made the club possible in the first place—only served to heighten young Emmitt's feeling of being special. Even if at that age Emmitt already began to suspect he could never be the man his grandfather apparently was.

As a boy, for Emmitt those days had seemed to stretch out forever. First in the little kiddy pool. And after what seemed longer than he could possibly wait, the bigger pool where the older children and adults swam and that young Emmitt had been in such a hurry to get to. After another of those ever so long waits, Ted, the lifeguard and swimming instructor, took him in hand, teaching him the Australian crawl in much the same way he had just taught Robbie—until the day came when Ted held him in the water and said, Ready? And young Emmitt nodded his head when Ted said swim to your mother. Emmitt did, keeping his eyes on his mother waiting at the edge of the pool, her green eyes smiling at him from under the bathing cap she wore, and who in another moment was pulling him up out of the water, the both of them happy and proud and excited while behind him he could hear Ted saying, Good boy, and

Emmitt's mother saying, You did it—just as Emmitt, too, was pulling Robbie up out of the water in a bear hug now and saying, "You did it."

And Robbie, all wet and small in Emmitt's arms, yet full of himself as he asked, "I did, didn't I?"

"You sure did, buddy. That you did."

Then Robbie was out of Emmitt's arms, yelling as he ran up to his aunt on the beach, "Did you see me, Aunt Jane? Did you see me beat Emmitt in the race?"

Who said—her voice coming over the water and the sound of the kids having fun up on the jetty—"I *did* see you, Robbie."

And this was all the boy had to hear. For of course he wanted to race again. They did so, over and over again, until his aunt came down to the water and insisted it was time to go. As they came out of the water, Robbie holding Emmitt's hand, Emmitt didn't know who he was happier for. The boy or for himself for being a part of it.

***

In his initial exploration of Cannes—before Jane and her nephew came into the picture—Emmitt discovered a restaurant on the Croissette advertising the "Best American Cheeseburger on the Riviera!" He had told himself he would eat there one night before he left but hadn't done so. That night when Jane returned from Antibes, after getting Robbie to bed, they walked down to this restaurant for dinner.

The day had been a good one for Emmitt. The swimming and the boy's eagerness in the water. The memories of his own childhood brought back to him. The good ones thank God, and none of the bad ones.

Bad memories could certainly have ruined things for him that day. And being ruined by them he may have—despite himself—hurt the fun the boy was having. But they hadn't, and still holding those good memories close, Emmitt was hungry that night for food that reminded him even more of home. Of when his life was good and simple and not threatened by the truths of the world. The restaurant with the "Best American Cheeseburgers on the Riviera!" would work perfectly for that, he was sure.

Unlike earlier in the day, the air that night seemed heavy and still as Jane and he walked down from his place. The streets and sidewalks were empty—of people in cars or on foot, on their way to dinner, some other entertainment, or just out for a casual stroll. He had been wondering how much longer the good weather might last. With the night air heavy like it was he suspected it wouldn't be for much longer.

Thankfully the food at the burger joint was good and hot. After his first bite of cheeseburger Emmitt said, "I hate to admit it, but this is better than what you'd get in a lot of places back home." He looked at her across the table from him, the big burger in her pale hands out of place against the white tablecloth and their wine glasses filled with Pinot Noir. "Those damn Frenchmen!"

"Yes." Her smile, her eyes, were just the way he hoped they'd always be when she was with him.

After dinner, over coffee, she was quiet. When he couldn't stand it anymore, and when he asked if something was troubling her, he was surprised by her answer.

"You know, Emmitt, I like how you are with Robbie." She looked up from her coffee. "Very natural. Robbie really likes you. The swimming lessons. The races in the water today. He couldn't stop talking about it all the way home."

"Well, I'm glad. He's a good kid."

"It might not be my place to ask, Emmitt, but I'm going to anyway."

"All right," he said, and smiled. He wasn't sure where the conversation was headed but had a feeling he wouldn't be comfortable with it. "If you must, you must."

"Do you regret not being a part of your daughter's life? I mean, seeing how you are with Robbie and all, it just made me wonder. "

Damn but she could certainly cut to the quick of it all right.

"To my everlasting shame, the answer is yes." He tried to sound flippant but couldn't pull it off. "It's not something I'm proud of it."

He was glad the girl came around to refill their coffee right then— not that Jane had any intention of letting up on him.

"Funny, I was thinking about her—Emily—just the other night."

These were exactly the kind of memories he had not wanted to think of—or discuss—that evening. But he did. Found himself telling Jane everything. The letter from Eileen when he hadn't been married very long that told him about his daughter. How he had thought about going to meet Emily. But put it off. Until finally he had put it off so long he was embarrassed to go. He told Jane about those times of miscarriage and heartbreak with Dana that followed. His fears and misgivings during Dana's first pregnancy. The two more sad repeats of the whole damn business and how the results were always the same. Until Dana grew tired of it and gave up. The overwhelming sense of relief her surrender had given him. "Another thing I'm not proud of. I was afraid I'd turn out like my father." It was as honest an answer as he was able to give her. "That like him, when things got bad I'd bail out. Couldn't even see it at the time how I had already done just that. Bailed on my daughter. Just like he did with me."

The coffee in his cup had gone cold. But when he went to signal to the girl for more he thought better of it. He didn't really care about having more. Or being where he was at that moment.

"That's too bad, Emmitt," Jane pushed her own empty cup away. "But people make mistakes, you know. I know I certainly did. Your father might have had his reasons for doing what he did. He never tried to explain?"

"Would have been pretty hard for him."

He hated the bitterness in his voice.

"I suppose it would be hard for any parent."

"Doubly for him. He killed himself before I was born."

For the first time in their brief relationship Jane appeared to be at a loss for words, and like the bitterness, Emmitt hated being the cause of it.

"What about your mother?" Jane's eyes on his were kind and bright enough. Just not bright, or kind, enough to bring him out of where he had gone. "Surely she must have tried to explain what happened."

"She tried," Emmitt said. "Told me the war had done something to him. That he was sick when he came back and didn't know what he was doing. It seemed plain enough to me what he had done."

"I'm sorry, Emmitt," Jane said.

"Me, too."

"We'd better go."

"Yes, I suppose we should."

It had started to rain, lightly, when they entered the restaurant. Now it was coming down hard and instead of walking back to his apartment they took a taxi. The ride was a quiet one, a quiet broken only as the cab was pulling into the drive and Jane said, "No matter what, Emmitt, I'm still glad you're so good with Robbie."

"Yeah. So am I."

Like that first time she stayed over and was gone when he awoke, Jane left a note for him to find in the morning.

I'm sorry for bringing up bad memories last night. I hope you will forgive me. Thank you, though, for being so honest with me. I feel like I know you even better now. Love, Jane.

He was sorry, too. But the note was nice. And he had already forgiven her.

***

The sun never came out that day. Instead, Sunday dawned cool and gray with a light drizzle that by early afternoon was a hard driving rain coming in sheets off the bay. Emmitt was glad he got out early for coffee and croissant at the bakery. By afternoon, even with a raincoat, he'd had have a wet, miserable time of it. For the first time since arriving in Cannes—France for that matter—he spent the whole day inside, with coffee and his copy of *Swann's Way*. The phone ringing in the late afternoon startled him from a nap on the futon in the little living room. It was Jane calling, to see how he was making out on the dreary day and did he want her to come down for dinner that night? All of which he answered in the affirmative, adding that he had a chicken and Mediterranean rice from the charcuterie by the bakery. Bought on a whim the other day, he said. In case of an emergency such as this. If she brought wine they'd have everything needed for dinner at his place. Instead of having to brave the elements.

She was laughing as she hung up, saying she'd see what she could do. Picking up the book that had fallen on the floor while he napped, he thought how pleasant everything was for him even with the dreary day and the driving rain. Even though just a few years ago he'd believed his life was over—that he was just hanging around until he died.

The rain continued like that for the next three days. By the end of the second day Emmitt had come to the conclusion it was time to make plans for going home. But on the fourth day the skies cleared, the morning wet and shiny and clean after the deluge, and he thought how maybe a few more days might be left. Days of sun and good weather spent with Jane. Pleasant nights with her making easy love at his place with the windows open and the nighttime sounds of the city outside.

But around noon some kind of crazy wind started howling outside, coming down off the mountains surrounding the town, and blowing so hard against the walls of the apartment building that it rattled the windows and sliding glass doors to the balcony. While making a fresh pot of coffee he realized he'd forgotten the morning papers at the bakery earlier. Deciding to take a chance he went to see if any were still left. He must have looked confused when he stepped inside the bakery a few minutes later, for the lady behind the counter pointed outside and said simply, "Le Mistral." Apparently this explained it all.

Instead of going back to the apartment, with the newspaper tucked under his arm, he headed off the other way. He had been housebound for three days with the rain. It wasn't raining now, so crazy wind or not he needed to stretch his legs. Needed to see something besides the small confines of the apartment—confines that seemed even smaller when Jane wasn't there with him.

The stores, apartment buildings, and homes of the neighborhood provided somewhat of a shelter from the wind. An older woman, dressed in black walked up ahead of him, bent over and struggling against the wind. Other than her, Emmitt appeared to be the only one out and about that morning. When he came abreast of the Russian Orthodox Church he felt—and saw—the full force of Le Mistral, as the lady in the bakery had called it.

Inside the church's open courtyard the palm trees were bent by the wind at a dangerous angle. Plants ripped completely free of the ground rolled like tumbleweeds across the cobblestones. Leaves from the oaks, and other trees, blew as well across the courtyard and gardens. With the sky all gray, the cold wind, the trees bare like they were, it was as if he were walking on a winter's day. Instead of one in early October.

Reaching the intersection with the Croissette he crossed over to walk along the sidewalk above the beach. The bigger boats moored out in the bay were gone now, the empty mooring balls bobbing up and down in the white-capped water. A few smaller boats were still tied up at the docks extending out from the marina at the northern end of the boulevard. Apparently the owners of these boats had left them to their fates. Emmitt didn't see how it could be a very good one. Not with the wind, and the white-capped waves lashed at them, banging the boats against the wooden docks until it seemed both docks and boats must be smashed to pieces.

He walked until he'd had enough of it—the driving wind, the gray sky, nothing of this day anything like the good days preceding it. He ran across the boulevard and into a café on a corner where he had stopped once before. The bright circle of neon in the glass door—a wine bottle, glass, and the words *Open,* lit up inside the circle, after the gray day and howling wind—were all the welcome he needed.

While drinking an Irish coffee and reading the paper, he sat at a little table by a window and watched the effects of the wind on the street outside and the bay beyond. When he felt like it he would catch a taxi back to the apartment. When he felt like it he would figure out what he was going to do about making arrangements to go home.

As it turned out, he wasn't alone in making plans to go home.

"There's something I should tell you, Emmitt."

They lay together in the little bedroom after dinner that night, naked, the covers pulled up against the chill of the evening and the crazy wind still howling outside, Emmitt thinking—before Jane broke the comfortable silence—how perfectly nice everything was right at that moment. Of how great it would be if it could just go on and on. Her, him, even the crazy wind blowing outside. Their bodies warm and at peace against that wind after making love.

"So tell me."

The wind picked that moment to howl even harder, if such a thing were possible, shaking the window in the bedroom and the glass sliding doors leading to the balcony.

"I'm flying home this Saturday."

"It's funny you say that." He sat up against the wicker headboard, gently pulling her up with him. "But I was thinking to catch the train back to Paris. Maybe on Sunday." He leaned over to kiss her. "I wanted to see what your plans were first. Before I made my own."

"I've been putting it off. The leaving. *And* the telling you."

"Kind of how I felt."

"God knows, I don't want to go," she said. "Would much rather stay here. With you. My father's not well, though. It seems he's been having a series of little strokes, TIA's or something like that, they're called. We have a nurse that comes and checks in on him three times a week, but I'm getting the feeling that might not be enough anymore. Not after talking to him on the phone the other day. He just doesn't sound right. I want to stay, but ...."

"Yeah. I'd like to stay here, too. A lot. I guess the world dictates otherwise, though."

"What about us, Emmitt?" she asked. "Is this the end of it? We just go our separate ways. Thanks for the fun memories and all that?"

"I don't want it to be like that."

"You mean that?"

"Very much so."

"So what will we do?"

" Between the two of us we should be able to come up with something."

"Good!"

And then they were making love again.

***

By Friday their plans were made. Emmitt was to go west the Monday before Thanksgiving. To San Francisco where Jane would pick him up at the airport. After two days in the city seeing the sights, they would head up the coast to Bodega Bay to celebrate the holiday with her family at her father's house.

"I think you'll like my dad," she told him. "He has some great stories from his days as a young man logging in the North Woods. He'll keep you laughing."

"I like to laugh. Never been in the redwoods either. Sounds like a win all the way around."

From there? Thanksgiving holiday with Jane, her father Lars, and the rest of her family, maybe. Nothing was set. The two of them would see how all that went. Take it from there. It seemed a sensible way to go.

That night they went to dinner at the Italian joint down from Emmitt's apartment. Jane was leaving the next day, taking the afternoon flight to Paris out of Nice. The following day she'd fly out early from Charles de Gaulle to San Francisco and home. Sunday morning was Emmitt's turn to leave, to catch the train to Paris, stay over, fly out Monday morning and be home in Ft. Lauderdale that afternoon. After that, they would be apart from one another, separated by the continent lying between them, until the end of November.

If this Friday night was to be their last for a while, Emmitt wanted it to be a good one. He had eaten there a couple of times before and knew the food wouldn't be a disappointment, which made for a good start to their evening together. After seating the two at a table in the corner, the waiter asked if they would like to try a bottle of the local red. The *specialty of the house,* he said. Emmitt said that they would like to try the red, and when the waiter returned, and pulled the cork from the bottle, poured a little bit in Emmitt's wine glass, then waited politely for his opinion.

"Very good," Emmitt said. "Merci."

"You're welcome. Enjoy your dinner, Signore and Signora."

As the dark haired waiter went back to his place by the door Jane smiled. "He addressed me as your wife. Does he know something I don't?"

"Excuse me?"

"Signora is Italian for Mrs."

"Oh really? Well then, I like that." He paused, and then added, "Like it a lot as a matter of fact."

To his surprise her cheeks went red—as if to compose herself, she said quickly, "So, Signore, I have a question for you."

"Ask away, Signora."

"Are you trying to impress me? Hoping that by bringing me to a fancy dining place, entertaining me with expensive wine, I might allow you to have your way with me later?"

"The wine's not that expensive," Emmitt said. "And to answer your question, yes. One can always hope. As they say in Italy. And I imagine, here in France as well."

It was a good way to start an evening, he thought. The respectful waiter, the pomp and circumstance of the wine tasting. The easy banter between the two of them. The way she looked in her black evening dress, the thin strand of pearls around her neck just enough to highlight her pale skin, blue eyes, and that blonde hair sweeping across her forehead. A good start. Even if the next day was to be the end of it. Even if it was to be only for a little while.

Longer than I'd like.

Jane had never been there before but agreed the wine was excellent. She liked the décor of the little restaurant as well, especially the murals on the walls, brightly painted images depicting modern day Rome. According to Jane they were just right for the setting, with the red tablecloths and the silverware gleaming in the soft light from overhead. Emmitt had never put much thought into that aspect of the restaurant—had been happy that the food and wine were as good as they were. But it was fun for him to listen to her go on and on about it.

A mirror ran the length of the wall across from them, dividing the mural in half, another aspect of the place Emmitt had not really noticed before. Turning away from her once he caught their reflection in the glass. A handsome couple, he thought. This man in his early fifties. The woman in her late forties. Both of them with smiles on their faces and appearing happy to be where they were at that moment.

"Have you ever been to Italy?" Jane asked, after the waiter took their order and then disappeared into the kitchen. "I've always wanted to go. But haven't yet."

"Nope, never been."

"Would you like to?"

"With you? Most certainly."

"You're so cavalier about it. I just might take you up on that."

"I hope you do."

"Me, too,"

Once outside after they had finished their meal, she stopped him.

"Wait a minute, Emmitt, please. I want to take a picture of you in front of this lovely restaurant. Something," and here she smiled that little smile that did so many things to him all at the same time, "to remember you by as a I pine away the lonely nights until we are together again."

"You're a funny Signora," Emmitt told her as he stood under the red awning atop the doorway into the restaurant. "But be quick about it. I have plans for you."

"You just hold your horses, mister," she said as she fiddled in her purse. "This won't take long."

She found what she was looking for, a little camera that Emmitt recognized from her taking photographs on the beach. As for posing for a photograph, well, he wasn't one for picture taking, told himself that he preferred to keep the memories in his head. But he wouldn't say no to her. Not this night. Probably not ever.

She was wearing thin high heels that night, the practicality of which Emmitt had questioned, considering the distance to walk to the restaurant. "Don't you worry about me, sir," she'd responded. "I've logged plenty of high heel miles in my day."

Now she seemed a little wobbly on them and maybe only because of the wine before and during dinner. Stumbling as she backed up with her eye still glued to the camera she said, "Oops, I must be a little tipsy."

Right then her heel caught on the curb, and she would have fallen backward into the street except that Emmitt caught her by the arm. Except for the car barreling down the street towards her it would have been comical: the goofy look on Jane's face when she tripped. That turned to a frown with the screech of tires on pavement as the driver hit the brakes and slid past the couple, now safely on the curb. It was a close call, Emmitt thought, as he picked up the camera Jane had dropped when she tripped. The fragility of life—so easily taken for granted when there was no earthly reason to do so.

Backing up to them the driver—a younger man with a sort of Peter O'Toole look about him, obviously drunk, but concerned—rolled his window down and in a heavily slurred British accent said, "I say old chap but is everything quite all right?"

"We're fine and thanks," Emmitt told him. And to Jane, as the driver wheeled away, "I think that's enough picture taking for one night."

"But I never got the shot."

"You'll just have to live with it."

"I suppose you're right," Jane said. "I'll just have to live with it. I really wanted a picture, though."

Taking Jane by the arm Emmitt steered her up the street back to his place where he was sure it would be much quieter—and certainly much safer.

***

Only the goodbyes were left. Along with her sister—whose husband couldn't be there because of business—and Robbie, Emmitt saw Jane off at the airport in Nice the next afternoon. When they were safely away the sister dropped him at the station for the evening train back to Cannes. Alone, except for his thoughts, he ate dinner that night at a restaurant he had never been to before, wanting to avoid any place he had gone with Jane. Back at his apartment he packed most of his things and placed the bag by the door. He read himself to sleep, though it took a long time.

He made a final visit to the bakery in the morning for coffee and a croissant. When he was done, with a smile and a wave and an *au revoir* to the lady behind the counter, he crossed the street to the bus stop where he caught the 9:15 to the train station. From there it would be the 10:35 to Paris. And that would be it for Cannes. And all that had happened to him there.

Unlike the ride from Madrid to the Riviera, with its lay-over and change of trains in Marseille, the return trip was non-stop. Once past the sprawling port city the tracks turned northward into the countryside where fall had arrived. The crops had been harvested and rolls of hay dotted the landscape. Even the sky above seemed harsher than it had been along the coast, grim and grey and devoid of the rich light that had inspired so many French painters over the years—light that had lifted Emmitt's spirits as well after his time in the city.

He half-expected to see Jane in the club car when he went for a sandwich and a beer, and surprisingly, was disappointed when she wasn't. The only others there were an elderly French couple, their gray heads bent in silence over their lunch. Emmitt sat with his beer and the day's *Tribune* and tried not to think how it had been before. And of course that was not possible.

That night was a restless one for him. The hotel was close to the station, just a short walk for him in the morning to catch the early train to Charles De Gaulle airport. Oddly enough, the hotel was only a block from Sylvie's apartment. It seemed to Emmitt a lot longer than three weeks—the Friday night he had taken Sylvie up on her offer of dinner. And afterwards, finished with their meal at the famous restaurant, their walk along the Seine, and by the Eiffel Tower. The quiet taxi ride back to her place, where it was obvious to the both of them they would make love. No, not love. But sex.

Much longer than three weeks Emmitt thought over dinner in the hotel's dining room. Hard to forget, though. Being with her. The ride in the cab through the night time streets. And how it wasn't just him and Sylvie in the cab—but all the ghosts of his past, as well. No, that wasn't quite true. There had been only the one ghost. A ghost who had not haunted him since.

He slept for a good portion of the flight to Miami, worn out from his fitful night in the hotel. Lulled by the steady drone of the plane's engines, he awoke only when the plane began its final descent. As the skyline of Miami came into view, he wondered how things were going to go for him now that he had a life again.

Part Five: The Coast Road

It was a hell of a note all right. Jane's phone call the Saturday night before he was to head west for their Thanksgiving holiday together.

"I don't think you should come, Emmitt," she told him. "Not right now."

"Excuse me?" A polite question from him—and at that particular moment—he realized later, not exactly the proper response. But he was too stunned at the time by what she just told him.

"Dad's had a stroke. A bad one, this time. He's in the hospital but supposed to come home Monday morning. We—the family—have had to cancel all our holiday plans. I'm so sorry."

"Yes, me too." And after fully understanding the situation, Emmitt was able to ask, "Well how is he? And damnit, Jane, I am really sorry to hear this. How are *you* doing?"

"The doctor says he'll live. But he's paralyzed on the right side and can't talk."

He could hear the tears starting to come—felt near as empty inside as he had the morning in the hospital after the doctor came into Dana's room and gave them the results of the tests.

"As far as I'm doing," she continued, it very evident she was trying to control herself over the phone. "I guess I'm doing as well as can be expected. Carol and her husband have been with me and Dad at the hospital since it happened. That's been a big help."

"There's got to be something I can do. Shouldn't I come out there? Help you with this?"

"I want you here, Emmitt. I really do. And please don't think I don't."

"But?"

"Just not right now. Let me get Dad home. Settled in. When I find out more about what needs to be done … what I have to do and what to expect, then I'll know more. Maybe you can come out then. For Christmas?"

"Okay. If you think that's best." He wanted to argue. But told himself he wasn't that selfish, and repeated, "Okay. But if you need me. If there's anything I can do for you right now, please, you've got to call me. I'll be on the next plane out."

"I know you will, Emmitt." And she said again with a catch in her throat he could plainly hear, "I know you will."

"I love you, Jane."

"I know that, too, Emmitt."

They left it there for the night and continued to stay in touch with the phone and email over the next few weeks. The holiday season — Thanksgiving, Christmas, the New Year—came and went with no change in her father's condition. Emmitt did his best to hold on to the idea that things would work out. With Jane and him. That they would be together, at some point, and plan a future together. Less than a week into the New Year that became questionable.

"I've got to put everything on hold right now, Emmitt," Jane told him one night on the phone. "I'm all Dad has now."

"We've got time," he said. "I'm not going anywhere."

"That's the thing. I'm not either. The doctor says Dad will improve, sure, but only a little. The stroke did too much damage. Carol can't help. She has her own life. I can't ask her to help. Other than the little time she can spare on the occasional weekend when she comes up from L.A."

"I know," Emmitt said. Not that he did. But he wanted to.

"I'm sorry, Emmitt. I just can't make any promises now. Everything has to be day by day. I hope you can understand. This isn't what I want. Believe me."

"I know," he repeated. "It's okay. It really is."

"I'm sorry, Emmitt." And then she had broken down and was sobbing. "I'm so sorry."

"I am, too, Jane." Thinking of an old movie, and with an irony he didn't really feel, and regretted for a long time after, Emmitt said, "Let's look on the bright side. For now we have Cannes to hold on to. The rest will fall into place."

He wanted to believe what he told her that night on the phone. Wanted to believe it very much. And hated the part of him that kept telling him he was a fool. And that they had come to the end of the line.

***

For the next several days after this phone call Emmitt went through the motions of the day. He woke up in the morning at the usual time, 7:30, went to bed at night, though there was no set time for this. Though he tried to stay positive about the future, for the most part these days passed in a sort of blur. What he found surprising was how he really felt about the way things were turning out.

This moment came one evening when he was sitting on the back porch with a whiskey sour as the sun was going down. The gray of the fading afternoon was laced with the buzzing of night time insects coming out in the yard, along with the sound of his neighbors pulling into their drives after a day at work. All normal sounds—all what went on day in and day out in this neighborhood he had lived in for close to a quarter century and never really felt a part of. He especially didn't feel a part of it now. The surprise though, was not that he didn't feel in touch with the life going on around him. It was at how angry he was

As he got up to go make another drink he suddenly stopped at the entrance way to the kitchen. "All Things Considered" was wrapping up on the NPR, his next door neighbor was calling out to her Johnny to come inside and get washed up. It struck Emmitt like a ton of bricks that no, he was not angry at Jane at all. Who, after all, had put the brakes on everything. He was angry with himself, instead.

An anger he couldn't put into words right then. They began to come to him after he returned to the porch with the freshly made whiskey sour—which when he'd drank half of it he realized he didn't like at all. But the words were simple. He was angry at himself for forgetting the hard lessons he had learned over the years about men and women. Learned first with Eileen Hobart, who one morning had simply disappeared out of his life, not to be heard of again until more than five years later. And then with Dana, a woman he had truly loved, married, gone through much with, good and bad. A love, a woman, a life, he had thought would never end. And of course it had.

Things happened in life and then didn't happen. He could question this all he wanted. Be angry all he wanted. In the end it didn't matter.

He would wind up with Jane or he wouldn't. In the meantime he had to work with what he had.

With NPR finished for the day the classical station was playing Ravel's "Bolero." The music brought him back to Spain—to Madrid and the warm Sunday afternoon he spent at the Plaza de Toros. Sitting in the stands amongst the Madrilenos, drinking wine along with the others, as the splendor and tragedy of the bullfight unfolded, Emmitt had an epiphany of sorts. As the first bull was being dragged out of the ring and the judges in their high stand were rewarding the matador two ears. He remembered a morning at the Cut on Squanocket two years back. It was the same. Of how that morning when he had hooked into that big albie, and still riddled with guilt and sadness over Dana's passing, realized he was still alive.

Much like that morning at the Cut, Emmitt had sworn—once again—that he was going to live his life all the way through. And the rest be damned. It was painfully clear, as evening fell on South Florida months later and far away from that Sunday afternoon in Madrid, if there was ever a time for him to cling to that decision, it was now.

***

Howard Kamen's phone call from New York the following week interrupted the monotony Emmitt had settled into.

"Good news stranger," Howard's voice boomed over the line when Emmitt picked up.

"I like good news." It was eight thirty on a cold, rainy, Thursday morning and Emmitt was in the middle of putting coffee on when his cell phone. "Could use some good news as a matter of fact."

"Oh? Everything okay with you my friend?"

"Yes, for the most part." Emmitt hesitated a moment, debating how much, or how little, he might want to say right then. He opted for the little. "You know me."

"I do—which worries me sometimes."

The good news turned out to be that an indie publisher wanted to reissue *Three Men* which had been out of print for close to fifteen years.

"I can certainly use the money."

"Well, I don't know how much money will come of it. They're an indie press, after all, and one that hasn't been in business all that long. Still, some reviews will be written and your name will be out there again."

"Send me the paperwork then and I'll sign on the dotted line."

"I'm adding a PDF attachment on an email as we speak."

"Thanks, Howard. You're a good agent. Hell, you're a good friend."

"I am, aren't I?" And again, Emmitt knew how Howard's face looked right then, the same amusement, with maybe one hand pushing his graying hair back from his forehead as he smiled into the phone. "Speaking of being a friend, I haven't spoken to you—well yeah, Christmas cards and that besides—since your sojourn on the Riviera. How did that go? Even more important, did you meet any women there?"

"One," Emmitt answered, and then hesitated again before adding, "Nothing came of it."

"That's too bad, my boy, too bad."

"Yes it is."

After the call Emmitt sat at the little table in the kitchen with his coffee watching the rain sheeting down over his backyard, the rain gray and cold, and evidence that even in South Florida, February could be a nasty month. It struck him then that talking with Howard, other than the necessities of store clerks and the like, had been the first real interaction with another human he'd had in weeks.

It struck Emmitt then, how alone he really was.

***

To put an end to the recent monotony of his days, Emmitt finished his coffee and with the rain over, and the sun coming out bright and warm, put on his trunks, got in his jeep, and drove out to the beach where he swam hard in the rain-cooled water for over an hour. On his way back to the house he pulled into a 7-11 and bought an ice cold beer to celebrate—not only the reissue of his first novel, but his minor breakout back into life.

The next morning he did this again. Unlike the day before, the beach was crowded, for a weekday at any rate, what with school still in. But it was February, the height of the winter season in South Florida, and all up and down the beach off the Strip tourists had set up camp, Seeing the bright umbrellas, and chairs spread out along the sand, Emmitt couldn't help but think of Cannes.

It came on him hard and quick and un-wanted. To forget the memory rising up he ran down to the water, dropped his towel on the sand and dove into the surf, letting the rush of cold water, the feel and taste of salt, push away it as fast and hard as it came. Later, after the swimming, he sat on the sand, drying in the warm breeze coming off the water, and forced himself to focus on where he was—the familiar ocean in front of him, the famous Ft. Lauderdale Strip behind him, the tacky bars, the old and new, hotels. None of it really like Cannes at all and that was okay. It was what he had.

And he got through that morning.

***

The weather stayed un-seasonably mild for the next week or so and Emmitt went first thing to the ocean every morning. The water, the sun, the feel of the beach, being by himself, letting it all wash over him, made him feel alive—made him forget Jane. At least for that small amount of time.

The nights were harder for him. The cocktails on the back porch as the sun went down, the radio on NPR, and the day's paper in his lap that he read went only so far. For sooner or later, he would be alone in his bed where try hard as he might, he couldn't help but think of her. The sound of her voice, that trilling little laugh he'd first heard in the club car on the train to Cannes. The wide open smile on her face. Worse than that? The feel of her body next to his. Of the way she smelled, clean and fresh. And how after they'd made love, that smell was different, wilder in a way, raw and honest and complete. All of this came back to him at night.

The day before a cold front was supposed to blow in and spoil the good weather, on his way back Emmitt turned left, then took the first right, and drove down the little one way street that ran past the town's first cemetery. He was able to walk right to the Raines family plot. The white low marble bench, the word Raines engraved across it, shining in the sunlight on the far end of the cemetery led him there. Standing in front of the family marker, hair damp from the swimming, his skin still sticky with the salt the ocean had left on him, he stared down at the three flat granite plaques laid in the grass.

John Raines' took center stage, flanked on the sides by similar granite plaques, one for his wife, the other for his son—Emmitt's father. These markers didn't say much:

Sarah Doon Raines
Born Oct 2nd, 1897
Died Sept 7th, 1976
Beloved wife and mother

John Rowell Raines
Born March 10th, 1893
Died, Sept 4th, 1961
Beloved husband and father

 Hilton Lewis Raines
Born, January 20th, 1921
Died, September 24th, 1948

Below these dates, and what took Emmitt back, it said, "Greater love hath no man."

Emmitt knew what it said on his father's marker—had known since he was a child able to read. It had been such a long time since he'd read them, though. After learning how his father really died, Emmitt had refused to go with his mother to visit the grave on the special days she did so. The last time he had been there was when they buried his grandmother. Now, those simple words carved in the granite plaque jumped out at him—words about his father. A man he had never known. A man he had hated for as long as he could remember. Words that suddenly made him feel like crying, and that drove him from the cemetery.

Heavy, menacing clouds, moved in from the north that afternoon. By midnight the winds ripped through his yard and down the streets, driving a torrential rain before it. Emmitt wasn't prone to bad dreams—the last one he'd had, had been that night on Squanocket, in the fall shortly after Dana had died, when wine drunk and in a restless sleep she came to him, sweet and loving at first, and then just a shallow death mask, her voice asking him why he hadn't done more for her.

But that night, with the rain pelting against the windows of the bedroom, he dreamed that the graves in the cemetery were washing out. In their rotting coffins the people who lay dead were floating away on a rain-driven tide. Most of these dead people in his dream were faceless. Except one, who—as Emmitt tried to step back—rose up from his coffin. Turning a bony head towards Emmitt, this skeletal apparition, in a frail voice Emmitt could barely hear above the screaming wind, moaned, "My son. My son."

He awoke with the dawn, the rain and wind still pounding away outside, his sheets wet with sweat—his father's words still ringing in his mind.

With the bad weather there would be no swimming that day. The first of March was two days away, and what with the rain and the cold wind, that month seemed to be coming in true to form. After breakfast, Emmitt sat on his back porch with a fresh cup of coffee and read the morning paper for a while, and when he was done, a three month old "Atlantic" he had never gotten around to. The coffee, the newspaper, and the book reviews in the magazine, helped to push the cemetery, and the bad dream of the night, away.

Thinking to get another cup of coffee, instead Emmitt went to the roll top desk in his office, returning to the porch with a pen and a legal pad. By the time noon rolled around the rain had let up and he had a good start on a story about his grandfather and the time he defended a local sheriff in front of the Kefauver Committee. The charges against the sheriff were corruption, concerning his involvement in organized gambling in Broward County.

The rain and the wind out of the northeast were still there the next morning and as he had the day before, Emmitt sat on the back porch with the legal pad until he finished the first draft of the story. He was pleased with what he had written so far, even if it was still pretty rough.

There were some details about the case, and the Kefauver Committee, he needed to research on the Internet. Still, the basis of everything was there, in black and white.

Even better was the fact that other than the memoir about fishing with Huff on Squanocket, he was hopeful that his writer's block had vanished. No. he was sure the block was gone. Cracking open a can of Budweiser in the kitchen, Emmitt realized he was back to work.

By the first week of June Emmitt was well into a novel. For now, the Kefauver stuff wasn't a part of it—though he wasn't sure yet if it might be included somewhere later in the story. Instead he was focusing on the relationship between a father and his son and what happened to them, between them, before, during, and after World War II. The two protagonists, of course, were based on Emmitt's grandfather, John Raines, and Hilton Raines, Emmitt's father. It was a story he'd never thought to write—had only stumbled on it, in fact, one night when he was browsing through his mother's old scrapbooks and letters he had kept after her death. Within the pages of the scrapbooks and the old letters, between the photographs, newspaper clippings, and letters, two men began to emerge. Along with these men came the story of their times, how they felt about what was happening around them, how they felt towards one another, father and son, together, and apart, in a world that Emmitt had never known.

The work was going well. Yet by the end of May, and into those first days of June he woke up one morning, went to sit with what he had written the day before to type it up on the PC, and couldn't. The simple fact of it was that he was exhausted from the writing. The poring over of letters and photographs. From the emotions flooding through him every day he put words to paper. He had to put it away for a while—to walk away and re-charge. Thinking that spring striper fishing on Squanocket should be heating up right about then he fired off an email to Rory to see if that was indeed the case.

"Hey Emmitt," Rory Larsen's return email began. "The spring striper fishing here is shaping up to be fantastic. Why don't you come up for a week or so and help me out with these bad boys? Been pounding them on the right tide at the Middle Grounds, as well as along the beaches either side of Squid Point. Let me know, and ASAP!"

By lunchtime Emmitt had plane reservations booked for the following week. He reserved a room at the "Lamplighter Inn" as well. It was as easy as that.

The night before he was to leave Emmitt called Jane. Even after all this time the little cell phone still felt strange to him. Just another reminder, he thought of time and progress moving on. They had a routine of sorts of talking a couple of times a week and sending emails back and forth. But he hadn't spoken with her in two weeks. Probably because the conversations lately had been strained, ending with awkward goodbyes. The emails of late had been brief as well, as had the cards and letters they had sent one another. Another sign of time—and progress—moving on.

Robbie and his parents had been up for a visit, she told him. The boy had asked about Emmitt, had asked when he might see him again and go swimming. Her father was doing better. He could speak in short sentences, even though he got confused on occasion and lost his train of thought. The doctor said that if he kept up this good progress she could probably find a live-in facility for him soon. She had mixed emotions about this, but had to admit it would be nice to have her life back again. Even if that sounded terrible on her part.

"It doesn't sound terrible at all," Emmitt said. "Sounds very reasonable, if you ask me."

After more small talk, and with the conversation starting to drift away from them, Emmitt said, "I just want you to know, Jane, I haven't given up on you. On us. I love you."

"Emmitt," but she trailed off.

"You don't have to say anything, Jane. Just know that I mean what I said."

After saying their goodbyes, and while making a night cap of scotch and soda to cut the edge off the phone conversation, Emmitt wondered if what he had told her was true. He wanted to believe it was. Wanted that very much.

Late the next afternoon, Emmitt found himself on the ferry headed across Squanocket Sound to a place where so many of the best times of his life had been spent.

It was certainly a fine day for it, he thought. With Day Light Savings time, even that late in the day the spring sunlight still hovered over the Sound, brightening the tops of the waves rolling across from the Cape as the big car and passenger boat plowed through them toward the dock at Ferry Town. He hadn't been to Squanocket in June for many years. Dana and he had gone once, and been put off by the summer crowds swarming the narrow streets and sidewalks of the island. They had vowed never to go back that time of year and hadn't. But thinking of those long ago vows Emmitt had to smile. He had certainly learned the hard way "never to say never."

It was no good having thoughts like that. Not on a day such as this one, when just above the easy spring haze hanging off the coast he could see the white houses of Ferry Town on the bluffs looking down over the Sound. Behind the bluffs the spire of the old Whaling Church on Main Street rose up above the wood shake houses. This constant landmark had always brought a lift to his spirits when he first spied it as the ferry approached the island. Standing on the outside deck above the bow watching as the land came closer and closer, the spire of that ancient church did so for Emmitt once again.

In another few moments the boat eased into the pier, the diesel smell of the idling engines choking his nostrils while the noise of people on the boat, and those waiting for them on the pier, streamed into his ears. He turned and started for the gangway leading from the weather deck, stopping to look back one more time just before stepping through the doorway. There he saw the gangly, tall, form of young Rory Larsen in the crowds on the dock, one long arm shot up over the heads of the others and waving. The sight of Huff's son waiting for him on the pier brought all of his past times on the island rushing in on him in a flood of memories.

"It's been a while, Mr. Emmitt," Rory greeted him at the bottom of the ramp leading into the parking lot. "How are you, sir?"

With one sturdy hand on Emmitt's shoulder Rory's other reached for Emmitt's bag. The younger man's blue eyes, heightened by a shock of straw-like reddish hair falling down across his forehead, were as alive as Emmitt had always known them to be.

"I thought we'd settled that 'Mr. Emmitt' and 'sir' crap the last time I was here."

"Three years is a long time. I guess I forgot."

Rory led him up the pier, away from the gangplank and the crowds gathered around it, past the docks and the ticket station where all was cars parked, and the noise of hustling throngs on a weekend day in a tourist town.

"But you're right. Emmitt. We did settle that. Sometimes it's hard to get past my mom's teachings." The younger man frowned for a moment. "And Dad's." Then the frown was gone as quickly as it had come and he shouldered Emmitt's bag. "C'mon, and I'll walk with you up to the Lamplighter."

The people and noise thinned out as they got away from the honking taxis, hotel vans, and tourist buses. They turned on North Bay Street, Rory walking along purposely with Emmitt's bag slung atop his shoulder, Emmitt puffing a little as he tried to keep up. He was more out of shape than he'd realized. The daily swims—before the bad weather and the rush of words in his head—had been good for him physically. Mentally, too. But the weeks of working at his desk had certainly softened him up. The Lamplighter Inn was only a half mile up the street but for a moment, he wondered if he would make it. It was a very embarrassing thought—Rory seeing him in such a poor state.

Coming off the boat he had noticed the burned out shell of Huff's old bike shop on the corner of Dock and Main Streets. The one bedroom apartment above the shop had been Emmitt's HQ for the last twenty of his visits to the island. Now, only the gutted frame of the building was left.

"Damn shame about the shop," he said as they left the docks and charred remains of the store behind. "I hope the check I sent was of some help. I know it wasn't for much, but I wanted to do something."

"Yeah." The younger man looked back, by instinct, Emmitt guessed, knowing as he did what the bike shop meant to Huff's son as well. "Your check *did* help and thanks. Tided mom over until the insurance money came. I wanted to rebuild the shop—not so much to start the bike business again, but well, you know."

Emmitt did know—knew well that wanting pieces of the past to always be there.

"But with Mom needing to go into assisted living right about then rebuilding the shop didn't make much sense. Dad left some but not near enough. Plenty of folks on the island—knowing how tight money was for us—thought I torched the place myself."

Rory laughed, his eyes and smile lighting up like his father's used to, the way Emmitt had seen many times, either when the old man was catching big fish, or shore side over a cold beer in the dim confines of the "Dockside Bar" as he recounted a risqué tale picked up in his travels.

"Not that I didn't think of it a time or two. It was pure Providence, though, coming through for us. Construction's picking up on the island again, thank God, and I'm laying more tile than a while back. We'll be okay. Mom likes the home, too. Makes it easier on me and Jenna."

Emmitt had to smile; it was the longest speech he'd ever heard come from Rory. A grown man now, but who Emmitt couldn't help but thinking of as simply Huff's kid. A boy, quiet on the sidelines, always deferring to his dad.

"Funny, isn't it?" Rory continued. "How everything changes."

"Yes," Emmitt said. "It is."

An hour later he was checked into his room at the "Lamplighter," suitcase unpacked, clothes put in drawers or hung up in the closet, his fishing vest, chest waders, tackle bag, and rod case arranged neatly in one corner. The sun had begun its descent in the west as he sat in the room's one wing chair looking out the bay window at the harbor and Ferry Town light. Both water and lighthouse were glowing—almost iridescent it seemed to him—in the fading rays of the afternoon sun. It was probably his favorite time of day and he was in a good place to enjoy it. Thinking to enhance both place and time, he pushed away from the comfortable chair, left his room, and went down to the lounge where he knew from past experience a very fine martini could be had.

In another few minutes he was out on the verandah of the Lamplighter Inn, martini on the little table next to the wicker chair he sat in, and the first biting insects of the June night coming off the dunes stretching between the inn and the Sound made for a long day. At least the traveling of the day was behind him, now. The seemingly endless check-in lines at the airport in Lauderdale had been un-nerving, to say the least—heightened as they were by the armed security guards on patrol and TSA agents pouring through traveler's bags. It was a new age indeed they lived in. One filled with paranoia and distrust. And with good reason, sad to say.

The scene at the airport, followed by the three hour flight, and then the two hour bus ride from Boston out to the end of the Cape, and then the hour ferry boat ride across the Sound, all of it made for a very long day. He was glad it was over. Still, mellowed perhaps by the gentle bite of the gin and vermouth, Emmitt wondered suddenly where he went from there.

Life had been a series of crossroads for him. For all of us, he supposed. Dana's death had been the worst of them. Jane's brief appearance in his life? Apparently an ongoing question mark. One that—with the martini and the night breezes wafting over him from the sound—he could live with for now. Standing up from the wicker chair to go for another martini, he couldn't help but think how nice it would be if there were no more crossroads left in his life. Straight ahead, please. Any decisions to be made consisting of only pleasant choices.

***

"You all right, Emmitt?"

Rory's voice—faint, disembodied, in the pitch darkness of the night—drifted down from somewhere atop the dune they were trudging up.

"I'm fine," Emmitt called out.

"Not too much further. The worst is almost over."

The new moon was forecast for the following night, but for now the sky seemed empty, devoid of even star light, the faint dots covered by the clouds of an approaching front, was why they were there in the first place. This combination of oncoming weather elements would be good for the fishing, according to Rory. Which hadn't been too bad already, since he, and his friend Gil, had been *hammerin'* stripers there the past three nights running.

Well worth the walk, Rory had told him as they geared up in a gravel pullover at the head of a path leading into the dunes. It's only two miles. Mostly sand, a few rocks, but pretty easy. They'd be there, before they knew it. "The Rocks." A natural jetty jutting out from the beach that no one, but no one, ever fished. It didn't sound bad, Emmitt thought, as he slipped into his waders and boots and buttoned up the thick flannel shirt he wore against the cool air of the June night.

"It won't be too much for you, will it?" Rory asked, after explaining the way to their destination.

"Jesus," Emmitt answered. "I hope not."

Now, having finally reached the crest of the dune where he stopped to catch his breath, the two miles—loaded down as he was in the waders, tackle bag slung over one shoulder and fly rod over the other— seemed like the longest he'd ever walked. He thought back on the old days, back when Huff used to lead him five miles, or more, down Quahog Beach, chasing after blue fish and the false albacore that came in thick there in the fall. He was glad Huff wasn't there now, to see him plowing along in the loose sand.

A few more steps and the sand became firmer beneath his feet, damp from the receding tide. In another moment the light from North Chop raked the beach, the rocks of the jetty standing out harsh and foreboding in the bright beam. Just as quickly as it had come the light was gone and in the darkness he heard the quiet shuffling of Rory putting his tackle bag down on the beach and unlimbering his rod.

"This is the place." Rory laughed softly, his smile illuminated suddenly by the small glow of a miner's headlamp attached to the bill of the ball cap jammed down on his head. "Striper heaven, as my dad might say."

Rory had loaned him a clip light to put on his own cap, and clicking it on Emmitt tied a sand eel fly to his leader, comforted, for some reason, by the sound of waves slapping against the rocks to the right of him in the dark. And maybe because it was a familiar sound. Even if he hadn't heard it in a while.

Looking out over the water, dark as far as his eyes could see except for the white breakers small at his feet, Emmitt thought how fishing was mostly just an excuse. A reason to put himself in places, all of them beautiful, he wouldn't be otherwise. Not that he didn't want to catch fish. Far from it. And as much as he told himself he had no right to be disappointed when he didn't—and there were certainly times when he did not—he couldn't help but feel a little pang of regret when those times occurred.

Fortunately, so far this trip had not been one of those times. Over the last week, in fact, they had done well with the stripers. Better than he had thought possible. A friend of Rory's had loaned him his boat, and they spent big chunks of the daylight hours following the tides between the Middle Grounds and Indian Head Point. Here, on the shoals just off the deep water of Squanocket Sound, with the incoming tide and the winds from the north a good rip formed up. Cruising stripers came out of the deep to feed on the tiny squid caught in the currents of those rips this time of year. Facing the bow of the boat at an angle to the rip, when they spotted the squid shooting up into the air in a frantic effort to get away from the fish below, Emmitt—or Rory, if it was his turn—cast big orange poppers into the tops of the waves breaking over the shoal. More often than not the result of the cast would be a striper on the end of the fly line. These were big fish, too. Some of them ran twenty pounds or more. Hard fighting fish that peeled line off the spool, their gleaming silver backs just visible below the waves as they ran towards the deeper water. Between them and the blue sky above, cloudless and clear, gulls and other seabirds screamed and dove for the offal left behind by the other stripers feeding on the squid. Finally, when the fish was brought boat side and released, whoever caught that fish traded places with the man at the helm, and back they would go, to do it all over again.

Yes, it was good fishing. Fishing that Emmitt enjoyed going over again in his head as he sat out on the verandah of the inn with the evening coming on, a cocktail in hand, his arms and shoulders tired from fighting the fish, from casting into the wind with the ten weight rod and the big, ungainly poppers needed to catch the fish,—that good kind of tired. It came from doing something he enjoyed very much and that he did not get to do very often.

This was the first time they had come out at night. Emmitt didn't know a whole lot about night time striper fishing, had even strongly considered the idea of saying no when Rory called earlier that day and asked if he were interested in catching the "night time bite." He was glad now he hadn't said no. If Rory felt his dad would have approved of their mission for the night, then it must be good. Huff had rarely been wrong. Almost never as far as fishing went. At least, not in the twenty odd years Emmitt and he were friends.

Rory finished rigging his line and clicked off his light. "I hooked 'em hard and heavy right here the other night," he said. "Another twenty minutes and the tide'll be perfect, just into the rise. If you stand quiet and listen hard you'll hear 'em slurping up sand eels in the trough. Almost at your feet. Just cast out where you hear the slurps and retrieve it slow. When they take it, hang on! If you need more flies or tippet or anything just give me a yell."

"Where are *you* going?"

Emmitt didn't want Rory to think he had to sacrifice the best spot just so his father's friend could catch fish. There seemed to be plenty of room for the two of them where they were. Especially since no one else was even on the beach. Just then, as he was thinking how alone they were in that remote spot, he saw a soft yellow light down on the other side of the rocks. So much for being remote, he thought. So much for having anything good all to yourself.

"Don't worry about me." Rory laughed. Emmitt could picture how the younger man's face would look with that laugh. "I'll be up on the jetty. Gil, got into a huge one off the end the other night. His feet slipped, though, and he dropped his rod in the drink trying to catch himself. Gil's an oaf. I won't make that mistake. Have fun."

And then Rory was gone and Emmitt stood alone on the dark beach. For a while nothing much happened. Standing in water up to his knees he cast out past the surf, trying to get a feel of how the fly would turn over in the slight wind blowing into his face, of how it would feel hitting the water. It was a little disconcerting at times because he couldn't see the fly in the water. Or the line. Nor hear the movement made by either. Occasionally the sound of a soft grunt from Rory scrambling out on the rocks drifted his way. If he looked hard into the dark in the direction of the jetty he thought he could see the younger man's tall form moving across the rocks. But when the slight glow of Rory's headlamp came on, well away from where Emmitt had been looking, he realized he was mistaken—that it was only his eyes playing tricks on him in the dark.

He settled down after that, getting into a rhythm of standing quietly in the water as the light swells broke against his legs, casting repeatedly into the night time sea. It was all lift, cast, strip slowly, one, two, pause, one, two, until it was finally time to lift, snap line up, and out, of the water. False cast once, double haul, pause, then shoot the line forward, imagining, instead of seeing, the fly sinking into the water fifty feet beyond where he stood, before stripping line all over again.

Mid tide something changed. The night seemed to go quiet, or perhaps it was only Emmitt's hearing finally attuned to what mattered. Out in front of him came the soft sounds of fish sipping at the surface of the water. A loud yell erupted from the tip of the jetty and he knew Rory was on fish. In another moment he felt the slightest of resistance on his fly and instinctively set the hook. The water blew up in front of him with a splash of pale phosphorous against the dark, the rod tip bent toward the shimmering eruption as his first striped bass of the night hit the fly.

They came on strong then, mainly small fish in the four and five pound range and that Emmitt enjoyed catching. The first explosive jump of the small stripers when hooked was the best part of the struggle. Unlike the bigger stripers, the schoolies tired quickly, allowing themselves after a brief battle to be hauled in to where Emmitt could bend over and thumb them out of the surf, admiring the silvery, phosphorous covered fish in his hands before releasing it back into the sea. The moon, out from behind the clouds that had covered it up, was full and bright, lighting up the shoreline, the dunes behind Emmitt, and the rocks, where Rory, out on the end, was a shadowed figure above the waves crashing against the jetty in the pale, surreal light.

With the fish feeding heavily like they were—and even better, taking the fly readily—Emmitt lost track of the time. They had left the Lamplighter at ten o'clock, driving in Rory's old pickup for twenty minutes or so to the east side of the island. Another hour maybe to hike the sandy path up and down the dune to the beach. That made it close eleven thirty, Emmitt figured. It was probably around midnight, or longer, before the fish turned on. So that when a lull came in the action he supposed it to be pushing two in the morning—realizing all this as he paused before casting one more time to where the slurping sound of feeding fish had been but now was quiet. Realizing as well that he was suddenly tired. Tired, an image of the cozy confines of his room at the Inn, taking up more and more space in his thoughts.

"Goddamn!"

Rory's yell echoed off the jetty and dunes, a harsh jolt in the night snapping Emmitt from his reverie of the warmth and comfort of his bed at the Lamplighter.

"Goddamnit, now!"

Emmitt heard the scraping of boots on the rocks and in a quick flash of moon light, before a cloud shut it out, saw Rory scrambling along the jetty toward shore. In another moment he was hiking up the beach. When he drew closer Emmitt saw the jagged pieces of broken fly rod Rory held in one hand.

"So that's what all the cursing was about."

He felt bad for the kid about the rod. Even if a part of him was glad for this sudden end to the evening, tired as he was and ready to leave.

"Must have been one hell of a fish."

"Yeah. It was."

In the glow of Rory's cap light Emmitt saw the sheepish smile on the younger man's face turn to disgust.

"Damn Derby rods. They used to give out good ones for prizes. But the last few years they ain't been worth a tinker's damn. I won this one just last year and was skeptical of it from the start. I know the Derby folks need to keep costs down here and there. But this one," and he shook the broken pieces in his hand, "lost me one damn big bass. Maybe the biggest I've ever seen."

"Damn," Emmitt said. "Now, that *is* a shame."

"Yeah it is. Not to mention I have to tell Gil. After I ragged on him about blowing his shot at a big boy last week."

He laughed as he clicked off the cap light and started up toward the dune, Emmitt trailing along behind him.

"Things get broken I guess," Rory said. "Bad timing is all."

"Yes," Emmitt said. "That they do. But, what the hell. Christmas is right around the corner, and I won't be here. Let's go to Sherm's in the morning and pick out a new rod for you." He smiled, even though he knew Rory couldn't see it in the dark. "My treat, kid."

"That's a nice thought, Emmitt, but you don't have to do that."

"Yeah, I think I do."

"Appreciate it, Emmitt. Thanks."

Isn't it always, Emmitt thought as his feet sank into the first soft sand of the dunes. What Rory had said. Bad timing. Broken things. And very little anyone could do to change it. Except try. And hope for the best.

***

It was a good fishing trip and Emmitt was sorry to see it end. The weather was mild with temperatures in the low 70's during the day, high 40's at night. The air turned even cleaner and fresher by the steady winds out of the northeast blowing along the New England Maritime making for a perfect respite from the cloying heat of South Florida in June. A cloying heat Emmitt knew would only get more so as summer went on. Still, all good things come to an end, Emmitt told himself as he packed his bags the night before leaving.

Making the leaving a little easier was the fact of how the fishing had changed over the last few days of the trip. The tides were later in the day, now. Not only that, the annual squid run had petered out, two factors making the stripers harder and harder to come by. With the looming July 4th holiday the island would be overrun with tourists, both on the shore and on the good fishing grounds. No, it was time to go while the going was good.

On the last day of June, a Sunday, Emmitt took the Cape Air shuttle from Squanocket to Boston, caught the afternoon Jet Blue flight to Miami, and just like that, was home.

He picked up where he had left off. He swam in the ocean first thing in the morning. Then it was to his desk, and the stack of pages that had waited patiently there for him while he was gone. His working title for this novel was *One Father, One Son*, and he worked on it until mid-afternoon, taking only a short break for a sandwich and a beer. No matter the word count, or where he was in the story, by mid-afternoon, when the words came harder and harder to him, he saved what he had written and clicked the screen off.

Another cold beer on his back porch as the hot summer afternoon peaked, whatever book he was reading at the time, a short nap on the futon , and his working day was over. What remained for him were two cocktails, the day's papers, usually filled with dire headlines about Bush's war in Iraq, and sometimes a third cocktail. Emmitt had decided his earlier feelings about whiskey sours were wrong and that they were actually quite good. He had a simple dinner, the evening shows on public radio, more of his book, all of this enough after the day's work to take him into sleep.

He hit a dry spell in September. When one day in the middle of that month he suddenly flashed on the train ride from Spain along the Mediterranean coast. How he had looked up from the Herald Tribune and noticed a woman sitting by herself across from him in the club car. And from taking these thoughts further—to those times when they were together. Swimming with the boy. And the better times. When they were alone in his little apartment above Cannes, making love while the breezes off the Med blew through the open windows, cooling their bodies slick with sweat. And how he had told her he loved her. And all that followed. The good, and the not so good. And of having to be patient until she was ready.

But he made it through those few fitful days of restless and un-productive memories. Enough so that by the first week of November he emailed a PDF of what he considered to a complete novel to Howard Kamen. And then sat back to await Howard's response, and the revisions he knew would be demanded of him.

All during these months of work, and rest, and everything in between, two constants stayed in his head. John Raines, Hilton Raines. Emmitt's grandfather and his father. Two men he had not really known. Men, with the help of his mother's scrapbooks and the letters they had written, along with the words he had put down about them, Emmitt believed he *had* come to know. As much, anyway, that was possible now so long after their deaths.

When the writing was done and he looked back over the printed pages, it struck Emmitt how fortunate he had been to have one of those men in his life—even if for only a little while. The other side of that coin—of course—how very sad it was that the other man had been no part of his life at all. A war, and the PTSD Emmitt's father had come home with, had seen to that.

There had been a third constant. One every bit as important as the two men he had written about. Jane Singleton. The women he loved and was not with.

***

One thing that kept coming back to pull at him—that cut at what Emmitt felt to be a well-deserved sadness over his father not being in his life. Emily, the daughter he had fathered with Anna Hobart. And that just as Hilton Raines had done with his son, had never bothered to know.

It was true he had sent a check every month to the post office box in West Virginia Eileen had set up. Never missed one, in fact, even during those times in the early going when money was tight. There was one time, when he simply had nothing in his bank account to draw on, that Dana had somehow come up with the cash. And that had really eaten away at him for a while' The look on Dana's face when she handed the money to him. Not bothering to answer when he asked what it was for—but gave him a tight smile and a shrug of her shoulders that said everything that needed to be said.

At least Hilton Raines had an excuse for his absence. He was dead after all. But for the whole of the thirty years, Emily Raines' father was very much alive. And this drew Emmitt up short, as well. Was Raines his daughter's last name? Or Hobart?

All of these pulling, churning, thoughts about his daughter came to a head a few days after he had sent the novel on to Howard. It was a Friday night and feeling that he owed himself some sort of celebration, Emmitt had gone to a restaurant on the Causeway known for its good steaks. Never one eager to eat at restaurants alone—especially since coming home from France—still, the thought of the mouth-watering fi-let mignon, and reeling in that glow of satisfaction the finishing of a long project, Emmitt took the plunge and went.

A couple, perhaps in their mid-thirties, along with their daughter, were sitting at a table across from Emmitt's booth. While enjoying the first sips of the Manhattan the waitress brought him, a girlish burst of laughter from the table derailed his thoughts of the manuscript. Looking over he saw how the man and his daughter seemed to be enjoying some joke, while the mother—who wasn't laughing—sat with a tight smile on her face.

"C'mon Mom," the girl said, tugging at her mother's arm. "It was funny."

'Yeah, Denise," the father chipped in, "It was just a little joke. A funny one, too, if I say so myself."

"It was really funny," the girl agreed, her eyes going back and forth between her parents.

"Okay, you two," the mother finally said, the tight smile on her face opening up a little. "I guess it was sort of funny."

"That's the spirit, Denise" her husband said.

"Yeah, Mom, that's the spirit."

Nothing unusual, Emmitt thought, as the waitress returned with his order. Just an average American family out to dinner on a Friday night. Everything good in their world, the three of them sharing a meal, all of them happy, and living their lives as the proverbial family unit.

The family at the restaurant stayed with Emmitt all the way through his dinner, on the way home, and as he sat out on the back porch with a nightcap. Nursing the drink he thought of Jane. Of Robbie. The times on the beach in Cannes they had shared. The swimming. The silly jokes he and Robbie played on Jane and that she always pretended to be mad about but really wasn't. The laughter they had shared. The look on Robbie's face when he beat Emmitt to the water on that first race. And how Emmitt was glad he let the boy win. And then Jane that night telling him how she really liked the way he was with her nephew. And then asked him if he regretted never being a part of his daughter's life.

Suddenly, Emmitt got up, went to his desk and fired off an email to Eileen Hobart. An email that—once the courteous preliminaries were done—requested all the information she could provide about Emily. How he could contact her. If Eileen thought that Emily might be okay with that. But that he really wanted to do so. And hoped with all his being that Emily would want that, too. And if not, he would understand. That he would understand if Emily wanted no part of him.

He had a hard time sleeping that night—was still awake as the first light of dawn came though his bedroom window.

***

"Well, I like it."

Howard's voice over the line was firm and sincere and Emmitt knew he meant what he'd just said.

"That's a relief, then."

The call came on a Tuesday morning, a week after Emmitt had sent the file to Howard. Emmitt was just coming in the house from his morning swim when the began to ring. Dropping his towel by the door, and still wet from the ocean, he hurried to get the phone, for some reason certain it was his agent on the other end.

"Of course, it needs some work," Howard went on.

"I figured."

"Nothing you can't handle, I'm sure."

"I'm glad one of us is sure."

A dry, hacking, cough interrupted Howard's chuckle—a cough that did not sound good to Emmitt.

"Are you okay?"

"I think so. My chest has been funny lately, sort of tight and probably because I'm getting old."

"You're not that old, man." Hell, Howard was only five years older than him. Sixty. In this day and time sixty wasn't considered old. The new forty hadn't he read somewhere? "You need to get that cough checked out."

"Christ, you sound like Mary. It doesn't suit you." Howard chuckled again at his little joke, this time minus the hacking cough. "But listen, Emmitt. That stuff about your father in the Philippines?"

"Yes," Emmitt said, unsure now where Howard was headed.

"It's very powerful, Emmitt."

"Thanks Howard. Thank you very much."

"I have to tell you I'm not fond of that character's name, though. It holds me up every time I come across it."

"Milton? I thought it was perfect. Should I change it to, say, Howard? Will that flow better with you?"

"You're a funny man, Emmitt Raines. But don't make me laugh. I'll start coughing again. We can discuss any name changes later. It's not that important right now."

"It was hard writing about him, you know?"

"I imagine it was, seeing how you've felt about him all these years."

"I was wrong about him, Howard. Really wrong. Reading the letters he wrote to Mom about the war, even heavily censored as they were, researching PTSD in the men who came back—still, that shook me. And then letters my grandmother had written to her after he died? I wish I'd read them before. When I was younger. Man, I just didn't know." And again, "I didn't know."

"And now you do?"

"Yes." A long pause, and then, "Now I do."

"I'm glad to hear this, my friend."

"Something else," Emmitt said.

"Okay. Tell me."

"I've been in touch with Emily."

"Your daughter? Really?"

"Yes. We've been emailing. Eileen gave me the address. No phone talks yet, but I'm hoping that will be the next step. Just figure to give her some time, you know. But we've been tossing around the idea of me coming for a visit. Sometime after the holidays."

"Well, I've got to say again Emmitt, but I'm very proud of you." Howard started to cough but managed to cut it off. "So listen—as soon as my notes are in order I'll send them along. In the meantime, I'm hoping you'll consider coming to my place for the Christmas holidays. I know Mary and the girls would love to see you, damned if I know why."

Unable to help himself Howard, was laughing, Emmitt waiting for any minute for that awful cough to start up and grateful when it did not.

The holiday invitation wasn't a total surprise to Emmitt. He had spent time during the Christmas season in the past with the Kamen family. When Dana was alive, but not since. He was probably overdue for a visit. Dana had enjoyed those times, being with a big family along with all the holiday trappings. She had especially enjoyed being with Howard and Mary's daughters. An enjoyment Emmitt had observed, more often than not, with bittersweet emotions running rampant through his head.

'Thanks, Howard," he said. "It's a nice offer, but how about for New Years instead?" He didn't know why he didn't want to go for Christmas, other than the fact he didn't want to. "We can bring in the new year with a bottle of your expensive Scotch and talk about all the good things the New Year will bring."

"My Scotch, is it?" Howard started to laugh, began to cough instead, and cut both short. "As you wish. Let me know your travel plans and we'll talk then."

"Yes, we'll talk then."

***

But they didn't. Emmitt went to New York after Christmas. Not to catch up on old times and ring in the New Year, though. Instead Emmitt went to New York to bury his old friend. On Christmas Eve at 5:20 in the afternoon, Howard left Macy's with an armful of last minute Christmas gifts and died in front of the taxi stand on the corner. Struck down by a massive heart attack, he crumpled to his knees, still holding onto the gifts he'd bought. According to the off-duty cop who was doing security for the store, the cop did what he could — administered CPR while waiting on the ambulance he called. To no avail for Howard was pronounced dead at the hospital before Mary could make it there from their home in Brooklyn.

She called Emmitt on Christmas Day just as he was finishing dinner. He had spoken with Jane earlier in the day, and though nothing was said explicitly, for some reason he had taken hope from the call. So much so he had driven over to the Jewish deli on the corner of 17th

Street and US1 and bought a Cornish hen and other fixings for a holiday meal.

Now, after Mary Kamen's call, he left what remained of the meal, taking only the glass of wine he'd been drinking, and went out on his back porch to process what Mary had just told him through her tears over the phone.

Howard's dead, was the first thing she said. Followed by, I'm sorry, Emmitt, I didn't call sooner. There were just so many people to call. He told her he understood. Not that he was sure he understood anything at that moment—not after hearing that a man who had been a good friend, not only that but as close to being a father for him as he had ever known, had died.

He asked about her and the girls and was there anything he could do for them. They were holding up, Mary said. All of them were together for the holidays, thank God. The funeral was to be on Friday, the 30th. He was still planning to come? When he answered, of course, she told him he was more than welcome to stay with them at the house. That had been the plan, after all, before this … and here she broke down and said, I can't believe he's gone, Emmitt, and Emmitt said it was okay, that everything would be all right—all the meaningless words that people said in these situations.

He told her he would see her the day after tomorrow when he got into New York, ending the call with, I'll be there as soon as I can, Mary. Neither of them said Merry Christmas, or any other holiday greeting. Just, I'll see you then.

And that was that. Like so many things in life, he thought, as he decided against the wine he still held in one hand, opting instead for a Scotch in honor of his friend. He wondered, as he raised the drink to his mouth, if he had thanked Howard often and sincerely for all he had done for him over the years. Emmitt really hoped that had been the case.

***

Howard was buried on a Tuesday, the day before the end of the year. The morning was cold and brisk, the wind, and ominous clouds overhead from a system coming down from Canada, making the day seem even grayer. They came early, almost an hour before the service was to start at eleven, the five of them bundled up against the cold as they walked the two blocks from the Kamen house to the church. Though a car from the funeral home was available, Mary had wanted to walk. "It's what we did on Sunday morning," she told Emmitt. "All of us together and I think Howard would want it that way today. Especially today."

Inside, the church was warm and softly lit, somehow comforting, Emmitt thought, as he sat in a pew three rows back from where Mary and the girls sat up front. He had never been inside a Catholic church before, so this would be his first mass of any kind. The light, diffused through the stained glass windows, the alter, choir stands, and organ bench, all seemed so majestic to him as he sat quietly in his pew, eyes focused on the coffin containing his friend on the funeral bier below the alter.

He hadn't thought of it until then—there had been no reason to—how Howard had converted to Catholicism to marry the woman he loved. "A very, very, small sacrifice, my friend," he'd told Emmitt years ago, when somehow the topic of religion had come up. "I never really thought of myself as being a Jew, didn't grow up in an observant household, so it just wasn't ever a part of my thought processes. Other than the occasional taunts of boys at school—taunts I settled with my fists. So when Mary told me her folks were appalled at what she was about to do, I didn't give it a second thought. Just said, well damn, what if I convert? Oh man, the look on her face right then. To see that look, hell I would have converted to cannibalism if it would secure me that look."

Well, that was the way Howard was. His wife, his family, meant everything to him. One of the reasons, really, that Dana had always felt so at ease when they visited the Kamens, coming from a large family like she had. An ease Emmitt didn't quite share, who was never good with more than one or two people around at any given time.

He thought of Huff once, as the priest droned on and on above Howard's casket. He hadn't been able to make it to Huff's funeral. Dana had been too sick to travel at the time and there was no way Emmitt was going to leave her alone. He knew Huff would understand—Mrs. Larsen even told Emmitt so when he talked to her on the phone. He regretted not being there but was grateful to be at Howard's service now, with Howard's family. Glad he could be there to say goodbye to a man who had done so much for him. A man who had meant so much to him.

The trip to the cemetery was almost as long as the mass. Emmitt rode two cars back from the one carrying Mary and the girls, with three other people he didn't know. Once there, he was glad to be out of the car and in the brisk cold of the day, away from the cloying heat of the car and the strangers he'd ridden with.

The sun had come out briefly from the gray mass overhead as the cortege entered the cemetery, a white statue of Jesus by the gates welcoming all who came there. A good sign, the sun coming out, one Emmitt thought he could see reflected in the tight smile of the woman sitting next to him, a dear friend of Mary's from school as was revealed on the long ride. The finality of where they were said all there was to say. His good friend was about to be offered up to heaven. Dead as Howard was, no portents, either good or bad, seemed necessary.

Emmitt left the Kamen house early that evening, once the last of the mourners had cleared out. He had booked a room at the Warwick Hotel downtown and planned to spend two nights in the city before flying out the day after New Year's. When the driver of the cab he'd called blew the horn outside, Emmitt was ready at the door with his bag.

"It just seems silly, Emmitt," Mary told him as she hugged him goodbye. "Spending that money on a room when you could stay here. The Warwick? It's so expensive, especially this time of year. The girls and I love having you. I'm more than happy to drive you to the airport, as far as that goes, too."

"You've got plenty enough to do as it is, Mary," Emmitt said. "I'll just be in the way."

The truth of it was that he wanted to be alone in the city where he had first met Howard. Back when his first novel was to be published and everything seemed to be there right in front of him. Instead, to make his leaving more believable, he told Mary he had never seen the ball drop in Times Square. That he had told Howard—before what happened—it was his plan to do so since he was going to be in town anyway.

"That's funny," Mary said, "but he never mentioned that to me."

"He must have forgotten. He was so busy, what with the holidays coming up and all. You know how he could be this time of year."

"Yes," she said, a strained look on her face that made Emmitt wish he could take back what he'd just said. "I do … know how he could be this time of year."

He slept well that night at the hotel. Despite all that had gone down the last few days. Perhaps it had something to do with the plush king size bed, the quiet simplicity of the room. Whatever the reason he was asleep, almost as soon as he shut the light out, a little before midnight and glad of it.

Emmitt had stayed at the hotel once before. He was twelve years old when his mother decided to expose him to "some culture," as she put it. It was his first time away from home, other than sleepovers with pals, or to his grandfather's ranch in Jupiter. It was his first time in a city bigger than Fort Lauderdale, as well as in a hotel. The museums his mother took him to were okay. What he really enjoyed were the two plays they saw on Broadway. "Camelot" because it was all about King Arthur and the Knights of the Round Table. "Irma La Douce," and mainly because of the scantily clad women on the stage and the risqué jokes that he vaguely understood—enough at any rate to know they had something to do with sex.

Just the act of checking in at the hotel, all just the same as he had remembered, brought back that good time he'd spent with his mother there. Back when he was young and his life secure.

In the morning he did the continental breakfast the hotel offered free to its guests in the dining room. If the rolls and Danish were a little stale, the coffee was steaming hot, and the fruits fresh. It was the last day of the year. His last living friend was now dead and buried and Emmitt had no idea what waited for him down the pike. Yet, he felt well rested—and alive. Unlike Howard, cynical as that might sound, may he rest in peace.

Like the day before, the morning was briskly cold and gray. Emmitt was glad for the overcoat he'd bought at a men's store at JFK. He would have been miserable at the cemetery yesterday without it. The weatherman on the TV in the dining room called for more of the same: a high in the mid-40's but with the wind, a chill factor of 35. It was definitely not South Florida winter weather Emmitt thought as he exited the hotel and headed up 54th towards the Rockefeller Center. Turning the collar of the overcoat up around his neck he was snug and warm against the wind, and curious to see what the last day of the year held for him.

The huge Christmas tree at the plaza was unlit that time of day. Even so, it added holiday spirit over the skating rink where, even at that early hour people, men, women, children, and teenagers of both genders, glided across the ice.

"They look like they're having so much fun." He turned at the sudden voice at his side. A woman, perhaps in her seventies, wearing one of those ludicrous Christmas sweaters that people only dared to go out in at that time of year, was watching the skaters below. "I love coming down here when the skaters are out," she continued, despite Emmitt having said nothing in reply. "Reminds me of when I was young and dating Ivan—before he popped the question—and we would come here to skate. Oh, I was so terrible at it. But Ivan taught me. He was such a good teacher and so patient. With everything."

She was lost in her memories and Emmitt wasn't sure she wanted him to reply. Deciding it probably didn't matter if he did, or didn't, he continued down Sixth Avenue. He had memories of his own after all. Ones she couldn't help him with. Just as he couldn't help her with hers.

Not everyone in the city had the last day of the year off. All around him people hustled in and out of the stores and office buildings lining both sides of Sixth Avenue. Buses, cars, delivery trucks, rumbled along the street, their exhaust fumes clouding the air with that distinct smell of city traffic. The noise of the traffic, the exhaust fumes, the steady drone of people moving all around him, seemed trapped by the walls of concrete riding up from the street. To escape the sudden cloistered feeling he ducked into a coffee shop on the corner of 52nd Street. The hot coffee helped. Just being inside, looking out the glass window at all that life flowing by outside, helped. In a little while, fortified by the caffeine and his short break, he felt like he could step safely back out into that city flow. He walked up 52nd to Seventh Avenue, then down to Times Square.

It wasn't the Times Square of his youth and that visit to the city with his mother. The garishly lit neon marquees over the porn shops, peep shows, and strip clubs Emmitt had noticed coming back at night when "Camelot" was over—and that his mother had safely steered him away from—were gone. It looked like the Mayor's efforts to clean up the infamous area were panning out. Instead of the bums, pimps, junkies and other riff raff, city workers were preparing for the night's big events, business people coming in and out of the buildings housing their offices, shoppers browsing the various stores, had replaced the square's former denizens.

The wind seemed to have picked up, blowing hard and cold down the street. On the corner opposite him now, a tall, completely glass-walled building stretched up from the sidewalk, and filled the whole corner. A young couple leaned up against the glass wall. In their late 20's, Emmitt figured, wrapped tight in each other's arms, this young couple was kissing. As he watched, two black dudes, probably the same age as the couple, came around the corner. "Yo," one of the dudes called out as he passed by the couple. "Get a room." He punched his companion in the arm, and laughing, the two of them went inside the store, the couple still kissing, apparently oblivious to anything, or anyone, except themselves.

Locked in their own time and place, Emmitt thought. Their whole lives stretching out untouched in front of them. Would they still be together through all that time? Still in love, still wanting to hold one another as they were now, uncaring of the passing world around them?

Emmitt had thought that would be the case once. For Dana and him. And it was, all the way to the bitter end. Funny, he thought, as he side-stepped two city workers putting barricades in place to block off traffic from an incoming street. For such a long time after Dana's death he had believed there was nothing left for him in the world. He didn't think that way anymore.

Something had forced him to leave that way of thinking behind. But that wasn't quite true. Not "something." But someone.

Another blast of cold air rushed down the block. At that moment the young couple broke off their embrace, and hand in hand, walked on. As they turned the corner at the end of the street and disappeared Emmitt knew what he had to do.

***

A week later, on a Friday morning Emmitt Raines woke up in another hotel, on another coast, a block away from the trolley stop to Fisherman's Wharf. The flight the night before had been long and boring. Not only that, due to a three hour delay in Charlotte it was late getting in. Why he had to go to Charlotte to get to San Francisco was beyond him. But there were no non-stops, this flight was cheap, there were seats available, and he'd gone ahead and booked it.

The good news was that arriving late at night in San Francisco as he had, even with the time changes, by the time the taxi from the airport dropped him at the hotel he was beat. Exhausted, he fell asleep immediately, sinking into the clean sheets, not tortured at all by nagging doubts of his plans for the next day that might otherwise have kept him awake.

Three cups of coffee, along with some watery scrambled eggs and dry toast, he was out the door of the hotel by nine o'clock in the morning. The girl at the front desk directed him to the car rental garage next door where she said his car was ready. It was, sort of. The attendant, a young Asian man with a sorrowful look to him, informed Emmitt there had been a slight screw up in the bookings. He had a car the gentleman could have, if he wanted, a red 2000 convertible Mustang a friend at another agency down the block had loaned him as a favor. Would this be all right for the gentleman?

It most certainly was—lousy color beside the point—and twenty minutes later, following the road map the sorrowful attendant gave him, as well as the attendant's directions, Emmitt was on the other side of the Golden Gate Bridge, turning the Mustang onto the Pacific Coast Highway and heading north.

It could have been fun to stay in the city a day or so and see the sights before going where he was going. If he weren't alone and on a mission he would have. If someone, say like Croc or Bosco, were with him he would have stayed and then some. Especially back in the days when he hung with those two. In the early 70's Frisco would have been a Mecca to them, with all the promise of drugs, music, and women the town was famous for. The three of them had talked here and there about going to Frisco to check out the scene. Like so much of how it went back then, they never got around to it. Of course, by the early 70's the whole hippie scene was dead. For that matter, Bosco and Croc *were* dead—Bosco for sure, and Croc? Last Emmitt had heard from Croc he was headed for India. This had been 1978, maybe 1979. No word had come from his old friend since. With Croc it was easy to assume the worst and Emmitt had.

But as he left the city behind him he was glad he had nixed that idea. The city wasn't going anywhere and he needed to stay focused on what he'd come all that way for. A fog rolled in off the Pacific as he was leaving the city. Though it was barely pushing 50 degrees he put the top down, enjoying the cool dampness of the morning as he drove. Tossing his duffel bag into the back seat of the car at the garage, he'd spied a CD lying on the seat. The Grateful Dead's Greatest Hits. Not a band he had ever listened to much, but considering where he was—especially after his thoughts of Croc and Bosco, and the high, happy days of their youth—perhaps the found CD was a karmic touch for his mission. Putting the CD into the dashboard player, he turned the volume up loud and pushed the car up to 60 mph, fog be damned.

Though he had Jane's address in Bodega Bay written down in a little notebook in his pocket, he didn't have a clue as to how to get to her father's house. He would stop at a gas station, or a convenience store once he got to that town and ask someone. It was a small town. Surely someone would be able to tell him. He hadn't called to let her know he was coming. Though he had let that thought roll around in his head all that week before leaving Lauderdale, in the end he passed on it. With all that time on his hands in Charlotte he had almost called her from there. But he hadn't called—instead he was on his way and there was no turning back.

Now, winging along the coast, the Pacific Ocean below the highway to his left and that he could not see because of the fog, he wondered at what the look might be on her face when she saw him standing on her front stoop.

The song blasting from the CD was something about a band by the river. Of seeing the light and having things to talk about.

Yes, they surely had some things to talk about. Jane and he. Many things. Mostly about getting it right. Sharing the pain and joy of being in the world. Of being in this world together.

Funny—because for most of his life it had never been that way—now it would be up to him to get the ball rolling once she opened the door to his knock. He had come all that way, after all. He supposed he would say, "Hello?" To begin with. Yes. That would probably be the place to start.

The rest could follow from there.

About the Author

Gene lee has been writing poetry and fiction since he was fifteen. Over the years his poetry has appeared in The Kerouac Connection, Cathartic, The South Florida Poetry Review, and other literary magazines. In his late forties he turned to fiction and began working on the stories and novellas that eventually became the Raines Family Trilogy. The three books that make up this trilogy, *Men Without Hate*, *Raines in the Day*, and *Emmitt at Love*, have been published by All Things That Matter Press. His outdoor stories have appeared in Sporting Classics magazine. An avid outdoorsman Mr. Lee enjoys fly fishing, wing shooting, and a gentlemanly game of gold on occasion. At present he lives with his wife of forty years on the banks of the Indian river Lagoon, where, when not writing, he can probably be found chasing the snook and redfish who roam those waters.

9 7 9 8 9 8 7 1 2 9 6 8 5